concrete flowers

GLOBAL AFRICAN VOICES

Dominic Thomas, editor

concrete
flowers

Wilfried N'Sondé

TRANSLATED BY KAREN LINDO

INDIANA UNIVERSITY PRESS

This book is a publication of

Indiana University Press
Office of Scholarly Publishing
Herman B Wells Library 350
1320 East 10th Street
Bloomington, Indiana 47405 USA

iupress.indiana.edu

Originally published in French as *Fleur de béton*
© 2012 Actes Sud

English translation
© 2018 by Indiana University Press

The paper used in this publication meets the minimum requirements of the American National Standard for Information Sciences—Permanence of Paper for Printed Library Materials, ANSI Z39.48-1992.

Manufactured in the United States of America

Cataloging information is available from the Library of Congress.

978-0-253-03559-2 (pbk.)
978-0-253-03560-8 (web PDF)

1 2 3 4 5 23 22 21 20 19 18

To Anna-Maria C.

… you never say a word, sometimes the sound that you
make, is like animals crying.

What if we were to take off together,
Toward a peace so tender and complete
And reappear from our ashes,
So beautiful, yet it makes me shiver!

concrete flowers

THE BASEMENT OF tower C, a long block of concrete, empty, unsafe, condemned and scheduled for demolition, is filling up little by little. Midway through the afternoon, the youth of housing project 6000 pile in, in groups of threes and fours, filling the dusty, smoke-filled setting of the makeshift nightclub Black Move. Spotlights hang from the ceiling, and all over the place are posters of stars you can hardly make out in the dark. Drinks are lined up on a plank held up by a sawhorse and chairs, picked up from the street. The room, previously used as storage space for bikes and baby carriages, has been completely revamped. Accessible from a steep stairwell, it is a short distance off to the right, down a passageway past the spot where they used to keep the—containers. You know you're there when you reach a door on which the barely legible inscription *Black Move* has been tagged with spray paint. The green, yellow, and red lettering form the shape of a clenched fist.

The girls and boys are ready to go, an expression of joy on their faces and their muscles flexed. The youngest are caught up in uncontrollable laughter, happy just to be there and have a good time. Predatory smiles cover the faces of the stars of the hood, hair carefully groomed and clothing meticulously chosen. The charmers are in the house, and they're looking pretty good, shimmying their way to the center of the room, cigarettes hanging from the corners of their mouths, on the prowl. The best dancers are standing apart, dressed in jackets in loud colors and sweat suits, the brand name proudly on display. Excited to show what they've got, they've come to try out and demonstrate their new choreographies.

~

The approach is measured, gestures are calculated, every step counts and becomes part of this precise scientific movement forward, has to stand out, especially in that crucial moment of making your entrance!

~

Everybody's checking each other out, standing around, greeting one another, hearts racing. High-fiving palms smack loudly; cheeks touch, kissing sounds, and guesses are being made about breast sizes under seriously tight outfits, pubescent and confident breasts pointing so high up they're swelling throats. The girls hold their ground, barely able to contain their excitement. There are dozens of stories to tell—love stories that only last a few days yet cause suffering for at least a whole week, hassles from parents giving them a hard time, fathers leaving and never coming back, mothers on the brink of nervous breakdowns—trying to trick their misery with three, four lies. The latest-fashion pocketbooks hanging on their shoulders, heels so high their ankles are at risk. Most of them wear excessive amounts of makeup because they've really come out to get some attention and show off their stuff. The teenage girls are all decked out for dancing.

~

Rosa Maria is ecstatic. The party is about to begin, the music and everything that goes with it. The ambience is warm, sounds to make you forget, enjoy yourself, far away from family, teachers, to hide and dream in secret, to feel nothing but giddy, enjoy a light sensation of dizziness, bubbles in the head, to chase away heart-breaking images, like the one of the recent death of Rosa's big brother, Antonio.

She lets herself go to empty her mind for a couple of hours. Mousy, awkward, and insecure, the teenage girl tucks herself away into the back of the room, invisible. She's going to have a good time, from a distance, too shy to put herself in the middle of the action and deal with the attention coming from everybody.

Rosa moves into the darkest corner and hoists her five-foot-two frame onto a shaky stool from which she can observe on the sidelines, slides her hands in between her thighs, and settles in to watch the party. Once again, she's come to admire Jason as he moves his beautiful body with rhythms coming from far away. She would gladly spend hours reveling in that, her eyes fixated on him. Seated, she hunches to hide her slight curves and cover up her face, which she doesn't really like. Rosa Maria doesn't consider herself particularly pretty with her black hair, jet-black, mid-length, curly, almost nappy, that she just lets fall in front. She even tries to conceal her thick eyebrows and dark brown eyes.

⁓

Black Move is packed. In the darkness, to the right of the entrance behind the veil of dust, you can make out DJ Pat, who's come expressly from Paris. His authority is indisputable. Apparently he was a huge hit in New York City. He scopes out the entire room with a confident look before zooming in on Rosa Maria, to whom he signals using his index finger. She buries herself even further into the weak light to avoid being seen, hiding her waiflike body and her face. Even while all eyes are on her in that moment, she declines the invitation.

Now focused on the two turntables in front of him, his baseball cap on backward, DJ Pat is in command. He gives the kickoff orders, and the crowd is holding their breath. The artist looks over his record collection one last time, double-checks his equipment, buttons, switches, needles, not forgetting the equalizer, low, mid, and high frequencies, and of course, the volume.

Bright lights go on, flicker ... Everything is good. He rubs his hands together, places a disk on the right side, raises the turntable arm, and lays the needle gently on the groove. The basement quiets, one more second, time suspended, dry mouths, balls of saliva easing down throats, adrenaline pumping and rushing through arteries, electricity running in the arm and leg muscles, heads bubbling over with excitement, awaiting the signal, the first sounds. The young people automatically pile their backs up against the filthy walls, leaving the dance floor in the middle empty, nervous, dying to explode, to let it all hang out, completely, to not give a damn and let go.

⁓

The DJ stands up. The moment is solemn. Beads of sweat glisten on his forehead, his concentration is at its peak. The record slides back and forth beneath his long, skilled fingers. You can hear the soft melody he's tweaking with different sounds. Suddenly, he just lets it all spin! The microgrooves begin their circular waves.

～

The attack. An offensive of decibels to the point of saturation, the bass so loaded you can feel your organs vibrate, your chest and body rise up. The sound level reaches its maximum, but the shrieks can still be heard. Bodies are shaking with joy, the excitement is palpable, fists are up in the air, girls, boys, everybody clapping in tune:

—Yeah! Here we go, it's going to be huge, the DJ is amazing, so massive!

The rhythm is vibrating so loud it could explode all the concrete in the projects. In the basement, after a whole week of keeping it together, about forty or more girls and boys are falling into a trance, feeling the urge to let it totally rip, far from all the daily frustrations, to roar with laughter, to let themselves experience the fever. It's party time! Their feet slide and hit the grime in carefully designed dance steps. Finally, a breath of relief, a hymn to life, the kids in the neighborhood are spinning around, jumping, creating new and outrageous choreographies in the polluted air of the basement:

—Show us your new style, your new *moves*, come on, let's go, show us what you got. Don't stop!

Arms in the air, going up and down, taking on new shapes, in harmony with legs twisting, opening up, moving in surprising directions, together creating a sophisticated aesthetic with original music, drums, bass, techno, hip-hop, reggae, zouk ... Everything goes into the mix, and the DJ raises it up a notch, it's gonna get pumping, it's gonna be lethal! At times, he stops the music to surprise the dancers, then he speeds up the beat, with storm warning sounds. The house is going crazy.

—Yeah, the sounds are way too cool. It's gonna be huge tonight. We're gonna give it everything. It's so amazing, the shit, man!

Nimble feet follow circles and curves, real geometry in a space overwhelmed by fresh bodily perfumes. Hips turn, going forward, backward, flirting with indecency, shoulders going backward, moving from right to left. The young people are letting off steam. The temperature is rising. The dirty damp walls perspire drippings of a foul stench.

Eyes keep looking around in the dark, and with the intense rush of hormones, pupils dilate, blood vessels are pumping and pulses are racing.

The girls are checking each other out, dancing, pretending not to care, and letting themselves feel desired from a distance. They provoke stares only to avert them afterward, juvenile games of seduction in the basement ambience. The boys look on without making themselves too obvious, careful not to miss their moment, a powerful aroma of charm is present at the party. The scent of sweat-filled pheromones overwhelms the atmosphere.

～

To stand out from the noisy and animated mass, some of them lean back against the walls, awkward, stiff and upright, smoking cigarettes. Among them is Mouloud, calm and reticent. The young man never dances. He spots Rosa Maria in the back of the room, goes up to her, and has to basically scream to be heard:

—Hey Rosa, how's it going?

—Cool, and you?

～

Without an answer or a smile, Mouloud tries to hide his discomfort in front of the young lady. He steps back, lights a cigarette, and settles about three feet away from her.

For a moment, he managed to distract Rosa Maria, otherwise hypnotized by Jason's elegance, as he wiggles and gets carried away by the rhythm. Attentive, she follows each and every move he makes. Rosa Maria is amazed, she knows all of his old moves and anticipates the new ones ... He dances even better now than he used to, more fluid and light on his feet. She admires the texture of his dark brown skin, especially when the drops of sweat trickle down, glistening on his temples, and continue down his neck. Rosa Maria is waiting patiently for the day when he will take her in his arms and make love to her, tenderly. Together the harmony of their bodies will create a gentle, languorous, and torrid vibration. Yes, the first time will be with him, he will only have eyes for her, and will whisper affectionately in her ear I-love-yous-you-are-the-only-one-for-me.

She has loved him ever since he came up all timid and afraid from his native Guadeloupe and thinks about him all the time. Jason had had a hard time getting accepted into the neighborhood. He had an accent when he first arrived that made everybody laugh. His family wasn't respected and was one of the poorest in housing project 6000. His mother, who raised him alone with his three sisters by doing housework anywhere she could, often had a hard time making ends meet. As a child, Jason was dressed any which way, and people ridiculed him and kept him at a distance. Rosa Maria remembers the tenderness she felt watching him keep a low profile in the neighborhood on his way back from school. At times, she used to console him when he would bawl his eyes out and rub them with his fists, after he'd been bullied or humiliated by the older boys.

～

Times have changed, and today Jason has made a name for himself as one of the best dancers in the projects, a good-looking guy with an irresistible smile, tall with broad shoulders, hair cut short, always in a way that flatters him, his slender frame supported by legs that never quit, in Rosa's eyes. He's sought after by all the girls and apparently by all the music video choreographers as well. Girls even come from neighborhoods on the other side of Paris just to watch him dance. At eighteen, the young man has become one of the stars of the projects. Due to the hours of weight training he never skips and the hours he's spent glued to his TV learning new choreographies, he now struts his stuff proudly, lets his presence be known. Chest protruding, his head is filled with ideas about the conquests to be made down in the basement. Tenacious and with great stamina, Jason had figured out, thanks to his performances on the dance floor, how to change his image and get accepted into the hood.

Miniscule, sitting in the back of the room, Rosa Maria stares at him, completely enamored. She appreciates the smallest detail and has convinced herself that they're made for each other, bound by some very special bond. She is totally consumed by this feeling and is certain that one day Jason will wind up recognizing the obvious, that he will open his arms and declare his love for her.

He's moving around on the dance floor and thrilling his admirer. Rosa Maria loses herself in her daydreams and completely forgets about the beating waiting for her when she gets back home. She knows her father will not miss the opportunity. He's forbidden her to go to the basement and can't bear the idea of her hanging out with the young people in the neighborhood.

～

Ever since the death of the oldest son, Rosa Maria's family has been living in turmoil. Antonio was found dead one morning in the supermarket parking lot. The garbage men had picked up the cadaver of an ageless man, ravaged by heroine, behind the shopping cart area. Naked, clearly stripped of everything by the homeless, his body had turned practically blue, his skin spotted everywhere with scabs from past shoot-ups, most visibly on the forearms. You could barely make out his facial features, his face washed-out as it was from the effect of the morning dew. He had to have been beaten up before he died; one of his eyes was nothing but a hideous violet-colored wrinkle that went from the bridge of his nose to his temple. The other eye, half open, sunk into a gray filthy hole surrounded by scratches. His hair had lost all of its brilliance, it was all caked together, dull, dirty, and hardly concealing the incredible sadness on his face. According to the medical examiner's conclusions, Antonio's death was the result of an overdose, and the police had wasted no time closing the case.

His mother, hysterical and in tears, had not been allowed to see his remains so as to spare her the horror of having to face her first child, unrecognizable, frozen in a pathetic pout, whose expression revealed profound agony.

Salvatore, the father, forever proud, had not opened his mouth. Standing close to the kitchen window smoking a cigarette, with a lost expression staring into space, he was even tougher and more uncompromising than ever. Salvatore had loved Antonio during his childhood more than anything but had wound up despising this smooth-talking useless son. He would throw in Antonio's face:

—Parasite, you don't work. I better not see you hanging around outside with those Negroes! They're a bunch of monkeys. You're just like them, lazy, good-for-nothing. There's no reason to drag your sisters into your schemes!

～

Salvatore had started worrying when he'd noticed that at around twelve, thirteen years old, Antonio was developing a passionate interest in literature and spending long hours immersed in novels, a world that was completely foreign to this factory worker. He would have much preferred doing odd jobs around the apartment with his son or both of them getting into blue overalls and lying on the asphalt parking lot and rebuilding a car engine. But Antonio showed no interest whatsoever in what Salvatore felt he should be passing on to his male descendant. Manual labor was boring for Antonio, a humiliation for Salvatore, and the more he read and studied, the more he spoke a French his father understood less and less. Frustrated, completely clueless about how to communicate and express himself, Salvatore was often irritated, and when he was short on ideas, he would immediately resort to beatings.

～

He would violently slap Antonio before telling him to take off his belt. Terrified, his son would obey and then tremble while bringing his hands to his face to protect himself. Antonio put up with it without ever daring to say a word. The wretched dance of the Native American belt buckle would begin. It would whirl in the air and brutally strike his skin, once, twice, becoming frenetic and interminable. Worn down, Antonio would clench his teeth and emit only stifled groans, louder and louder, his jaw tense and reddened face marked by tears and sweat.

His three sisters, Sonia, Rosa Maria, and Anna, hiding away in their room at the other end of the apartment, would bury themselves under the covers or nestle up next to each other and cry, in silence, so as not to stoke the paternal wrath. Angelina, their mother, expressionless, managed to swallow her tears by keeping busy doing housework, a zombie with a broken heart, practically jumping out of her skin every time the leather and metal of the buckle struck the skin of her firstborn child. She would hesitate but never step in. Salvatore was convinced that in order to make a man of his son, the dreamer with crazy ideas who didn't even contribute an income to the household, he had to be iron-willed. Antonio could very well play the intellectual with his friends outside the home, but at home, Salvatore was still the boss, and as the father, he had the last word.

～

Salvatore refused to attend the funeral of the wreck found on the asphalt somewhere behind the supermarket. When the police officers asked him to identify his son, he basically responded with a quick, contemptuous glance at the dead man whose face they revealed, before agreeing with a slight nod of the head. He left the morgue without saying a word.

The bus dropped him off in the city center, in front of the bakery next to the African hair salon. Worn down to the core, this family man went past the Halal meat market, weighted down in his stride, feeling dispirited, then sat at the counter in the café PMU, with his back turned to the huge television screen where the horse race had captured the attention of most of the other clients.

～

Tides of bitterness and sadness tortured him, a rush of images streamed through his memory: his immense happiness after hours of agony during the delivery in the maternity ward, the exhausted yet radiant face of Angelina, her emotion when the midwife handed her the baby, pink, crumpled-up features buried in a cocoon of white linen, a warm smell of cleanliness and milk, his tiny eyes, fists closed; his first smile, his faltering first steps toward his father's wide-open arms, the velvety kisses on tender, chubby skin, the feeling of pride during their first trip back to Italy after settling down in France. Then adolescence came, the misunderstandings, the contempt, screams replacing tenderness, the snapping sound of doors slamming, suggesting retreat and estrangement, voices screaming out, confirming the ever dangerously widening distances. The violence. Blows to the body as forms of caresses, childhood disappearing, hope losing its momentum before falling flat, lifeless on the dirty, wet asphalt.

～

Today, Salvatore is at the end of his rope. Laid off from the automobile factory where he worked for more than twenty years, a semiskilled worker, the system of three eight-hour work shifts, fingers broken, back thrown out.

Despite the strike, management had decided to go ahead with the inevitable debt-restructuring plan in light of the current economic crisis.

| According to the study made by an independent auditing firm, they would need to relocate to save the company. In the official statement sent out in the mail, it was about unfavorable circumstances for investments, deficits, early retirement for senior workers, and redeployment for the junior employees ... Back at home, this factory worker had a hard time finding the words to explain this disaster. Uncertainty hung over the family for several days. Seeing her husband heavyhearted coming through the door wearing a worried and evasive expression, Angelina felt sick to her stomach, her face appeared lifeless. Fragile, she placed her hands at the edge of the kitchen sink, the gray strands of hair fell forward when she lowered her head and began to cry. She turned her back to her husband, miniscule beside her, humiliated, defeated, stunned by the *coup de grâce* of his dismissal.

The shadow of long-term unemployment hung over Salvatore. Nothing would be like it used to be, no more summer vacations, no more long afternoons killing time at the café, frustrations every day, misfortune!

—Ah, the bastards, always looking out for number one, it's always the little guys and the poor who have to suck it up!

The union representative, red with rage, roared in the corridors. He'd checked in with Salvatore, who'd just left the office of the head of human resources, in order to slip an envelope with a couple of bills in his pocket.

—Don't worry buddy, your coworkers and me, we won't abandon you and the others, we're going to fight. Come on, take this, don't be too proud now, good luck... We'll go get a drink when you've got your new job!

◆

Wilfried N'Sondé

Lost in a confusing ballet of incoherent internal chatter, Salvatore is stuck in an impasse of inactivity, the wind knocked out of him. His production unit relocated somewhere in Eastern Europe. Forever silent, useless, watery eyes fixated, stuck, staring at his big, knobby fingers, idle, a question mark, Salvatore is slowly going off the deep end.

Idleness and the inability to meet his family's needs have emasculated him. The shame of having become unemployable, someone no one needs, chills the conjugal bed at night. Silence, filled with reproach and unexpressed thoughts, has lodged itself between him and his wife, created an abyss where the embraces and tenderness of their youth remain buried. The heart racing wildly and butterflies in the stomach of their first moments are now far away, a faint memory, a forgotten dream.

Salvatore's wife, exhausted from fighting a losing battle against the hardship of meeting month-end expenses that keep piling up every day, doesn't even allow him the caresses he can basically no longer lavish on her anyway. His virility is now a foregone conclusion, a memory from another time. Off-kilter, their family is falling apart. Angelina keeps her disapproval to herself. She expresses her contempt in the distance that becomes greater and greater between them over time. She's angry with him for having placed the burden of their material needs squarely on her shoulders. She alone takes responsibility for the humiliation of having to live on a life support system from welfare services, depending on handouts, joining the line alongside those abandoned by a consumer society at the Catholic Relief Services or at various other charities. Groveling, with a sickly complexion, lifeless eyes, old-fashioned cheap clothes, averting her eyes from the caring smiles of volunteer charity workers.

⁓

Salvatore ended up at the neighborhood bar, with a glass of red wine, the cheapest, at the counter, his expression sad and low, holding a cigarette butt. Beneath his eyelids, the nightmares of the belt marks on his dead son's body, the screams, but also the repressed longing for tenderness. In his fantasy, a need for affection, for gentleness in the touch beneath his fingers, of a sensitive caress delicately posed on his cheek. The scents of his youth come back to him at times; he dreams of someplace else, of a new spring.

⌣

Ever since her brother's passing, Rosa Maria no longer speaks to her father. His presence disgusts her. She can bear neither the sound of his voice nor his smell, convinced that he never really loved Antonio and never accepted that he was different. He'd killed Antonio with the relentless hounding he subjected him to. Antonio had left home prematurely to get away from Salvatore's constant harassment. His departure had created a huge rift between Rosa Maria and Salvatore.

⌣

At night, when she's in bed, the young girl jumps up the moment she hears heavy footsteps on the kitchen tile leave the window before going back to the bedroom.

A part of Rosa Maria died when her brother passed away in the back of the supermarket parking lot. Antonio, so kind, so dynamic with his jokes and his crazy ideas, always just the right words, cleverly distilled, impeccably dressed, white shirt and black pants held up by his faithful belt with the Native American buckle. He was the one who'd had the idea of investing in the big basement in tower C, which was no longer being used, to make a nightclub for the young people in the neighborhood, so that they could go dancing without having to pay, at least once a week:

—Too bad for the owners. We're going to show them we don't need anyone. Let's stop moaning and groaning and get to work! The police have no reason to come by and bother us. We have rights. We live in a democracy here, right?

Open up a club, this was his last great feat, a huge success. Antonio encouraged residents to take responsibility, to create opportunities for themselves, grab them, to not remain passive, to stop complaining and waiting around for the hypothetical government intervention to improve their situation.

Young people danced hassle free from the beginning of summer vacation; the authorities put up with it. As usual, the guys from project 6000 listened to Antonio, dubbed The Good Man. Everybody respected and trusted him ... The whole story about drug trafficking and overdose, nothing but lies and malicious gossip. No one believed it. Even today, the opinion is unanimous. Antonio was too clever for them, he was. It's simply impossible that he died all alone.

~

Rosa Maria tries to bandage her wound by loving even more intensely. Her feelings for Jason have become a real obsession. She's hanging on for dear life, a lighthouse in the storm, a glow in the darkness, a lifeline. In her eyes, he represents both reality and an opening onto a dream.

~

At Black Move, she devours him from a distance, her eyes riveted to his swaying pelvic movements. Jason intensifies the back and forth, the circular moves, slow, sometimes fast, convulsive moves, an erotic symphony accentuated even more by the expression on his face. He's closed his eyes and lightly bites his lower lip. A circle is forming around him, the others are clapping, they want more and are chanting his name:

—Jason! Jason!

Rosa Maria struggles to hold back the impulse to jump out onto the dance floor and cling to him, to wrap her whole body around him in his dance, to feel him close to her, her head resting on his chest, to blend in completely with his perfume. She's reveling in the moment, Jason is smiling with her, she's sure of it. He spins on his heels, surrounded by three admirers. African girls. Rosa Maria dreads them the most. For her, it's unfair competition, especially when they follow Jason in his choreography and can go along with the moves of his rhythm and keep him going. These girls show off proudly in the middle of the room with their great hairdos of ebony and blond highlights. Rosa Maria tells herself that they must have spent the whole night and a good part of the morning getting ready. She stares at the tallest, who also happens to be the prettiest one, the one they call Fatou. Rosa Maria has already come across her in the neighborhood, not that Fatou could even be bothered to say hello to her. A young woman of about five foot seven, brown silky skin, almond-shaped eyes with a delicately sketched face. A magnificent way of carrying herself, huge chest barely hidden beneath her plunging neckline, legs that won't quit, outrageous curves, and round buttocks molded into a pair of white jeans. Rosa thinks she's quite simply drop-dead gorgeous, perfect. She wonders how in the world Fatou managed to squeeze into those tight jeans that are so close to her body they're practically showing a bit of her lace underwear at the waist.

—Hey, you over there, what's with you looking me up and down like that? You want something or what?

Annoyed by Rosa Maria's fixed gaze on her, Fatou moves toward her, fire in her eyes, threatening. Drowned out by the loudspeakers, Rosa Maria doesn't hear the provocation, she just sees her rival coming toward her, shoving her way past the other dancers. There's total confusion, and things are heating up. Hunched on her stool, Rosa Maria is ready to get roughed up, unable to defend herself, resigned. She shrivels up into an imaginary shell. Jason pulls Fatou back, before she has a chance to strike, by grabbing her at the waist:

—Come on, it's OK, Fatou, let it go. It's Antonio's little sister, you know, don't be stupid, she doesn't mean anything, come on, it's not a big deal. Come, let's keep dancing, it's a party, isn't that what we're here for?

—OK, but she better cut it out. Next time, I'm taking her down, you feel me? You better watch out with your nasty face!

Jason is all nice and sweet, his voice is calm, he looks in Rosa Maria's direction with an expression full of compassion. He then takes Fatou by the waist back to the middle of the room.

—Cut it out, Fatou. Shit, come on, let's go dance.

They go back to the middle of the dance floor, and the party picks up, even better than before, feet in the dust, young muscular bodies shaking it up to Caribbean sounds. Alone in the back of the room, forgotten in her corner, her heart cramped, Rosa Maria just wants to disappear, she thinks about leaving, frozen in her steps, and goes back to her daydreaming.

~

Patient, certain that Jason will be her first, her cheeks blush. She thinks about that day with the sun on her irises. Her slightly curved

Wilfried N'Sondé

figure, her eyes black from routine sadness, a star will shine when Jason takes her into his arms! She'll be happy, the afternoons will look like those summers of some years ago now, during the last vacations in Sicily, the days when the factory used to sign checks at the end of the month and the whole family would return to their little village built on a hill. Salvatore was treated like the mayor. They were welcomed in a big celebration of hugs and an overwhelming outpouring of love. The elders would pick up the kids and spin them around in the air. The men would grab each other by the shoulders and agree in a man-to-man nod that clearly everyone was doing all right! On Sunday, the family and neighbors walked together in procession up the narrow path that led to the church, all cleaned up and dressed in white, the men, closely shaved, stood upright and dignified, while the women, especially the single women, took advantage of the uneven terrain to let their long shiny curls dance in the wind. They moved their hips slightly, dressed in their flowery skirts, never abandoning their radiant smiles. Then they would dine outside, a table of more than twenty people, a real feast of fresh vegetables, cold cuts, slices of salami, smoked ham, pâté, sauces, spaghetti, seafood. They stuffed themselves and laughed at Antonio's jokes; he was always charming, wearing a smile on his face. Everybody enjoyed him. Later on, they would relax and let the food settle, listening to melancholic love songs intoned by the women that they'd all repeat together, eyes half-closed. Salvatore paid for the wine and didn't even count how much they drank! In the afternoon, after the cups of black coffee, half the village enjoyed themselves on the beach. The little ones ran happily around every which way, sticking their feet in the water to splash their parents. The young girls would raise up their dresses thigh high to refresh and show themselves a little bit, an explosion of joy under the sunset, breathlessly running along the water's edge, the men sipping liqueurs. Sitting aside, mothers swapped stories about their problems all in good spirits. They were good together, as a family, happy.

Today, in the winter of unemployment in the heart of project 6000 tucked away in the Île-de-France region, amid a little bit of hope, there are fights, drugs, puddles of spit in the stairways, modern comforts in the apartments, young lazy boys sitting on half-broken benches or crowding into the halls of the buildings, talking, laughing, annoying other residents. Sometimes, their eyes beam with joy from being together, at other times, their eyes are gloomy and mean when boredom settles in. Teenage single moms forgotten by family planning. Social ascension for some. Racists. Police on the lookout. No cash flow, television every day to forget. The humiliation of accompanying moms to the child welfare office. The squalid waiting room, always so crammed. Infants crying … Impatient people who get all worked up at the counter. The poor, their arms weighed down by administrative documents, incomplete forms that no one understands. Educational failure. Gray hair, ugly faces of those who haven't succeeded. Social outcasts. Life keeps on going without them in magazines and TV commercials. Foul language scribbled on the walls next to the entrance doors. And especially Antonio's horrible and mysterious death behind the supermarket.

Project 6000 swallowed up the family, lost forever within high rectangular sentinels, enclosed like so many in human cages gridded by glass windows.

The commuter town took them in under its reinforced concrete blocks of melancholy and suffering, and holds them down on the asphalt. The projects provide lodgings in a functional apartment in the heart of a gigantic building with straight angles, constructed way too fast, to deal with the most urgent cases.

Rosa Maria stumbles around in the new tormented neighborhood still looking for its soul, disoriented. She makes every possible effort to flee the gloom and grasp a sliver of happiness by reaching for hope, however feebly.

By early evening, the party at Black Move is starting to wind down. Rosa Maria is thinking about Jason, but he's vanished. The crowd prevents her from seeing him. She silently cherishes the warm feeling comforting her and summons up her perseverance. It's a calling, the most beautiful of them all! For the two of them, she hopes they won't make love in the sleazy basement that smells of piss, decay, and lubricating oil. She imagines a huge bed, silk sheets, like in the song she heard when she was a child, when the king's horses drink in the middle of the bed, a bouquet of periwinkles draped on the bedposts, Beauty and the Beast style, if you know what I mean, and peaceful sleep until the end of the world.

To bring the night to a close on a high note in the basement of tower C, the music changes, the sound system releases a final series of romantic melodies. Far in the back of Black Move, Rosa Maria taps her feet nervously into the space below her sad throne, boys rush to ask girls to dance, last chance to score before heading home. Newly formed couples embrace each other, cling to each other, tightly, take over the dance floor and begin a ballet, their pelvises playing the lead roles, holding on to each other firmly in the low light and dust, blood pumping from being so close to another person's body, a frenetic waltz, swirl of fabrics rubbing against each other, inner thighs touching in step, sweat intermingling, the bass vibrating right into the heart revs up the excitement, electric shocks in the spinal cord, some sweet words, a few compliments risked in the brouhaha of the basement, the hope of seducing.

No one invites Rosa Maria to dance, but she doesn't lose hope. Jason doesn't notice her. He doesn't come to her. She knows he's *the* specialist in the art of gallantry. In the neighborhood, it's said that no girl can dance twice in a row with him and walk away with virgin lips. Abandoned, she coils up, her hands between her legs, chin on her chest; her beloved still hasn't approached her. A little lamb completely lost, afraid, terribly sad, it's an unfair game. She knows she's helpless, alone, without any particular appeal, transparent, a stranger to beauty, gives the impression of suffering permanent discomfort. The world has forgotten her! Still, she does not give up hope. And what if he actually came up to her, really close, took her by the hand and gallantly invited her to dance with him in the humble, charming style of the well-dressed gentlemen in the balls of the olden days that she so admires in the movies on television . . .

⟢

Her dream is here, right in front of her. He's kissing the beautiful Fatou on the lips, his hands are moving like crazy all over her back, her sumptuous hair sways with the rhythm of the kiss, the caresses go right under the T-shirt and then on to explore her belly and navel. At the end of the song, they both head for the exit, hand in hand. The crowd makes way for them, he's upright and as proud as a cock, she's shaking her rear end in the faces of her defeated rivals.

Rosa Maria bites her lip and is once again the little dreamer girl, two long braids on either side of her head, an old Sicilian lullaby playing in her ears. She sees her mother again, making her tender, measured gestures with her morning hairstyle before breakfast. Those were the first years living in the projects, when everything was brand new, when there was hope after all the tough times in Sicily, the departure for France, all the modern comforts in an area close to the Parisian periphery.

JASON HAS LEFT. Minutes go by and temper Rosa Maria's ardor. Her legs are heavy. She gets up and heads out with the others. The young girl crosses the alley of the railroad station; it's already nighttime.

Rosa Maria melts into the crowd of passersby rushing to get back home. She goes by unnoticed in the middle of the shopkeepers' rackets, selling off their final merchandise cheaply before closing up, poultry, fruit and vegetables, clothing in unseemly colors, of mediocre quality.

She tries not to think about anything as she's crossing the main artery of the housing project between the supermarket and the mayor's annex. Then she goes past the crossroads, with the huge multicolored flowerpot in the middle, walking quickly and quietly to avoid being noticed, on her tippy-toes, her head slightly leaning forward, hands in the pockets of her blue sport jacket, over jogging pants in the identical color, wide, a refuge for hiding her femininity, which is sorely lacking. Rosa Maria isn't precocious. She smiles while tightening her lips to hide a disgraceful set of teeth that she much prefers to wearing braces, which would make her a laughingstock at school.

On the concrete bench in front of her building surrounded by black wire fencing with several holes in it, Rosa Maria recognizes Mouloud. Alone, perched on the back of the bench, cigarette in his mouth, he takes a long drag before sending the smoke into the air, then spits a trickling of saliva while smacking his tongue between his lips, and remains in that position contemplating the ground, his legs spread apart and his elbows on his knees. Such moments of solitude take up most of his days, preoccupied with vain attempts to reorganize the disorder in his head. Distracted, he slowly turns around when the young girl comes up to him.

—You already here, Mouloud?

—Yeah, I got freakin' bored, I had to make a move. For a club it sucks … You know, Rosa, to be honest, your brother wouldn't want you hanging around there, you know that, right?

Pensive, Rosa Maria sits down next to him. Mouloud moves to make room and avoid physical contact with her.

—He would have understood my reasons. Antonio, he understood everything, you know that well enough. He was your buddy, wasn't he? Oh well, better head on home. I'm late, my father's going to kill me!

—Yeah, Rosa, you have to listen to your father, it's about respect, you know! Your brother's not here anymore, but you're lucky, you still have your father!

She hesitates a moment.

—Do you really think it was drugs that killed Antonio?

—Leave it alone, Rosa, don't try to go there. Some shit you just have to let slide. Even me, his homey, he didn't tell me everything. Think about yourself, let it go, don't get caught up. You're like a little sister to me. I swear on my mother's life, I got your back. I promise, you can count on me.

Mouloud gets up, stands up straight, in an official and dignified position, his chest upright with his right hand placed on his heart. Rosa Maria smiles and touches him on the shoulder:

—Thanks, Mouloud, honestly, you're so nice!

Mouloud also has his head down often. He speaks very little but spits a lot, a propulsion of little transparent bubbles at regular intervals, the result of a skilled movement between the teeth, the tip of the tongue, and the upper lip. In twenty-five years he's become a real master in this respect, it's second nature to him. His father had ordered him to do his military service in the army of the country of his ancestors, to avoid him turning into a sissy. Mouloud stayed for more than a year in a barracks in some far-off location in the desert somewhere in North Africa.

Since that time, the young man produces a maximum of twenty sentences a day. Over there in the desert, he learned the hard way that he was French. Trauma, abuse, bullying, blows, and daily humiliation. To avoid becoming the housemaid and the whore in his group, in a leap of pride, he reacted by hitting and biting, out of intense desperation, and imposing his will with the strength of his fists.

These days, there's a dryness in him, a kind of gaping wound that affects him mentally and partly impacts his normal ability to speak. Since Antonio's death, he feels more or less OK in Rosa's company, even if he can't express his feelings. At times, he concentrates for a while and then explains to the guys in the neighborhood, who'd never even dare to contradict him:

—You see, she's a nice girl. I respect her and all, you know. She doesn't pray, but she does the right thing, you feel me? She's nice, you know, on my mother's life. Plus, we're talking 'bout my homey's sister. Now that he's dead, I gotta watch out for her, you feel that?

He often avoids looking directly at her so that his eyes won't betray the compliments stuck on the tip of his tongue. He prefers to spit in silence and admire her when she's not looking.

Mouloud hardly ever smiles and never dances. He'll randomly beat somebody up for showing a lack of respect or giving him a funny look. His fists clenched so tight they could almost perforate the palms as he violently swings to strike the faces with a crash of bones and flesh, swollen skin, red knuckles, the impact of bodies falling to the ground, kicking in the ribs, screams of pain, stop, shit, stop! Your basic brawl, taking off long before the police show up. Mouloud is practically indifferent to pain. On his return from the army, he got closer with Antonio, who saw in him a young man alone and somber and took him under his wing. Mouloud listened to him talk with real fascination and followed him around like a shadow, proud to be his right-hand man.

～

Mouloud often sits on the bench listening to the others talk or watching them play football. The moment they start talking about girls, he gets uncomfortable and takes off.

—Anyway, they're all just a bunch of bitches, oh yeah, swear on my mother's life!

Most of them resolve the issue of love with about twenty or so euros, a little less for fellatio, more for extras, well, all depending on the means and the moods that day. Margarine, the blond with the big tits, forever wearing skirts that are way too short, waits for them in the basement of building F.

～

After a moment of silence on the bench, Mouloud turns toward Rosa Maria:

—You shouldn't waste your time at Black Move, it's too seedy for a girl like you. Antonio would never have wanted you moving in those circles.

—Yet he was the one who set up that club, he's the one who even negotiated with the electrician to turn the power back on.

—Yeah, but he didn't do it so that you would go there, he arranged it for the others. You remember when your sister wanted to show up the first time, how he threw her out? Now that he's not here anymore, look at the way they treat you, they don't even respect you anymore, the bastards. The whole thing disgusts me, you know, that's why I got out of all that shit, I swear!

—That's not true. Even Patrick, the DJ, recognized me, he waved to me, yeah. Everybody saw him.

—Patrick? He's a clown. Gimme a break!

He spits on the ground between his legs then raises his head toward her. Rosa Maria holds her hands together between her knees, shoulders pulled inward, rocking back and forth trying to get warm.

—He's gone, Antonio. For me, it kills me, I think about him all the time, I'm so sad. I have to enjoy myself, Mouloud, you understand. I'm still young after all, gotta live my life, you know ... and it's really for the music. When I listen at home, my father screams at me, he tells me to stop the savage shit. Well, look who's coming!

~

Fifty yards away, Marguerite, nicknamed Margarine, turns the corner of the middle school and heads toward the bench. Rosa Maria recognized her silhouette under the dim light of the streetlamp. Mouloud clenches his jaw into a pout of disgust then spits furiously to the left of the bench.

Rosa Maria calls out to her friend and waves at her to come over:

—Margarine, Margarine!

Margarine smiles, raises her arms in the sky too, and rushes over. Her long blond hair sways on her shoulders. Huge, intense, bright blue eyes illuminate her little pointed nose, which sits above her plump, turned-up pink lips. Every morning, she exaggerates their sensuality by carefully putting on dark red lipstick. Margarine, a pearl, stunning, one of a kind in the neighborhood. You can see her strutting up and down the little alleys in the hood, always happy, smiling, head held high with a big proud chest beneath, dramatically indecent flattering outfits. She walks in heels way too high that accentuate her voluptuous waistline and hips. She shakes her well-rounded rear end, a veritable moving temptation. She provokes and arouses desires. The young woman mesmerizes her admirers, makes men go crazy. Her generous curves and suppleness of a grass snake blows their minds. When she passes by, it's a hypnotizing spectacle for the male sex and a scandal for the women. Housewives curse her and barely hold their tongues, filled with insults of the lowest order:

—You not ashamed to dress like that? Slut, fucking machine, wait till you get old, whore, bitch in heat. Wait till you see your face when I get a hold of you!

~

When serious family men bump into her, they first tense up, and then they have a hard time swallowing their saliva. Margarine hypnotizes them, they go crazy in their pants, a moist and humid tornado in their routine and boredom. She opens them up to a forgotten and frightening universe, the raw desire to possess a young supple body and to lose their face in her ample bosom beneath her firm skin. One last chance for folly, to be intoxicated, the appetite for a wild ride, to forget and pant in cadence to the point of complete exhaustion, having traversed many skies.

When she left high school on her sixteenth birthday, she started her activities in the abandoned basement of tower F and has since serviced many with the power of her flesh. This is how she earns a living. A reasonable number of daily tricks to shelter her from being in need, in a discreet location below the building, a mattress covered in dark sheets, a small coffee table with a lamp that gives off a pale light, thus creating the illusion of mystery and privacy.

~

Mouloud is uncomfortable with Margarine coming over to them; he's clearly agitated:

—Why do you talk to that whore?

—Cut it out, Mouloud, she's my friend, don't speak so loudly. Even my brother really liked her, he left her alone, he used to say that we should respect her and not cause her any harm. It's not her fault, you know, if she's sometimes with boys, she wasn't lucky with her mother, who took off, and her father, who drinks like a fish.

—OK, Rosa, be careful with this slut … I'm outta here!

With one final spit, Mouloud crushes his cigarette and takes off. No money in the world would make him say hello to Margarine. A few minutes later, she arrives at the bench.

—Hi, Rosa, how's it going?

Four kisses on the cheeks, then the two young ladies hug each other affectionately, clinging to each other for a while.

—Cool, and you?

—Making do. What you doing hanging with that part-time Islamist? He's lost it, he freaks me out. Be careful, he's not working with a full deck!

—No, it's because you don't know him. He runs his mouth, but honestly, he's so kind, all heart, and really sensitive, I swear! And he's my neighbor, he lives two doors down from me. I've known him since I was a kid, you know?

—OK, it's your business, Rosa, but be careful all the same … Say, when are we going to take a trip, just the two of us?

—Cut it out, let's not even talk about it. You know as well as I do that things aren't like before.

—What, Rosa, weren't we good together the last time? OK, whatever. By the way, I saw your sister Sonia working on the checkout line at the supermarket. Did she leave school or what?

—Yeah, with my father unemployed and everything, you know, things are tough, so Sonia decided to make some money so she can help us out. With the housework that my mother's doing, we'll be in a better position to pay the bills, you know.

Margarine is taken by a fit of the giggles:

—Hey, tell her to do like me. We could share the basement. She would make a whole lot of dough. Oh yeah, I promise you that!

—I don't like it when you get like that, please cut it out! You liked my big brother, Antonio, very much, didn't you? I'm sure he wouldn't want to hear you talking like that!

Margarine pauses, her features freeze and become sad, her blue eyes become misty, clouded by bitterness. Tones of regret can be heard in her voice, fear too. She bites her lip, breathes deeply, and responds in a serious manner:

ı —Don't bring up Antonio anymore, Rosa, he's gone, that's all, there's nothing more to do, there's no point. It hurts, Rosa, when I think about him ... just don't, please.

For a moment, she disappears into the pain of a bad memory, her sad eyes look up toward the sky, sorrowfully recalling all the great moments she had with him right up until the tragic end.

—You know, Margarine, I think about him a lot. It's just not possible that he died all alone ... It's not possible, somebody did it. For me, that's how I feel.

～

Margarine exhales slowly like someone getting rid of a heavy weight on her chest. She turns toward her friend and adds in an exasperated voice:

—Forget it, it's the drugs, Rosa, it's really serious shit, this stuff, it makes people crazy. Even the best of them, like your brother, they don't know what they're doing after a while. Don't ever get into it, that's all! You know, Antonio had started hanging out with some shady characters, dangerous guys. That's what made him lose his way.

—How do you know that, Margarine? He talked to you about it? You sure he was taking drugs?

—No, I don't know anything ... I mean, I'm not sure ... He's gone, Rosa, let it go ... it's the kind of stuff that gets repeated all around ... They say he started using coke shortly after leaving home, you know, that's why you never saw it, he didn't want to get your family mixed up in it, Rosa.

—But why, shit, I don't get it ... Why?

Silence overwhelms the bench surroundings. Images of the past scroll by with the strong feeling of waste ... Everything was going so well when he was still there. Rosa Maria daydreams and sees herself sitting on her brother's knees again. He's tickling her while pinching her with his index fingers on the sides above her hips, she wiggles all around without ever really stopping him, the scene continues and drags on eternally. Every so often in her crazy movements, she touches his cheeks and enjoys the rough touch of his five-o'clock shadow growing in.

Margarine raises her head and clears her throat to erase the memories and regain a little bit of her countenance; a huge smile lights up her face. She breaks her silence and asks:

—By the way, your father's always standing by the window on the other side of the building, ogling me every time I go by. Honestly, he's so weird. He got a problem or what?

—Hey, don't talk like that, he's my father, you know. What do you think? He lost his son, that really shakes you up, you know, plus have you seen the way you dress?

—OK, don't get upset. I just wanted to tell you, that's all . . . OK, you're not going to start calling me a whore too and all the rest of it like the others? Stop, we're friends, aren't we?

—I apologize, sorry, excuse me, that's not what I was trying to say . . .

For Rosa Maria, Margarine is not merely the prostitute everybody takes her for. It's just that over time something fundamental has broken in her soul, and since then, she's been in the habit of waiting for men in the basement. She rents her body to them for a couple of dollar bills. She no longer feels anything; her flesh has become a stranger to her. Family men call on her services in secret, full of shame and perverse desires for this woman who could be their own daughter. Having drained their wives with endless frustrations and housework, they've stopped touching them and deplore the flabbiness of their bodies, betrayed by time. When night falls, they visit Margarine, a few crumpled bills in the palms of their calloused hands, heads down, their virility standing in line, a lecherous eye, moist lips, hungry for the corolla offered, fresh and pink. Of all of her clients, these are the ones Margarine despises the most, for their cowardice and hypocrisy. She's learned not to let herself become brutalized and knows how to tame their rough handling.

—Take it easy, dude . . . No, you don't get to kiss me!

These falsely dignified well-meaning patriarchs, tyrants of public housing apartments, disgust her the most. They ignore her in the streets and treat her like a princess, the mistress of their pleasures, in the basement. Margarine patronizes them as much as she can all the while eyeing them scornfully. The young prostitute has them by the purse strings. Indifferent, she expresses boredom under the weight of their brief and loud embraces.

—OK, go on now, others are waiting!

The client quickly puts his clothes on. Sheepishly, not so proud after the act, he avoids her gaze while she glares disdainfully at him in the darkness of the basement, ice blue shards beneath her pupils. Margarine clenches her teeth.

Once she's alone, she sometimes cries in silence without ever really understanding why, overcome by a vague longing to exist somewhere else, differently. All the same, she continues her business with disgust for the men and for herself, her skin defiled after the rough contact, unfamiliar, intimacy with something strange. She's losing herself by defiling herself over and over again.

To do her job with a minimum level of security, the young woman benefits from the protection of the tough guys in the hood, some old friends from nursery school who've become petty criminals. In her kingdom of the slums, she had deflowered every single one of them at puberty. They owe her particular reverence, some recognition, and subservience even. Margarine will always be the first woman with whom they discovered their body and came to appreciate its pleasures.

Antonio was her favorite. She really had it bad for him, a truly unique guy, special, so much gentler than the others, affectionate, often anxious and worn out. Lost between his father's beatings, the need to protect his sisters, and his plans for the neighborhood, which had, before they fell through, created a lot of enthusiasm among the young people. So much pressure under which he was falling apart. Not to mention the problems with the police lately because of the contacts that he did not willingly provide with some strange characters in Paris, men dressed up in suits and ties with strong foreign accents. One time, Margarine accompanied Antonio to a meeting. Following a brief greeting on the restaurant terrace, she had left them to talk business.

Margarine liked hearing him talk, going on for a while, using words like in a book, clinging to each other in the darkness of the basement. He dreamed big dreams, his eyes beaming, and she would hide the rawness of what she was feeling by closing her eyelids. Her cheeks would flush, and Margarine would relax. From the mouth of the man she would have loved to call her lover would come wild ideas about running away, countries to discover together, a whole different life, another world. No one had ever shown her so much attention and respect. The attention he gave filled her with satisfaction. In his gaze, she finally felt worthy. But as she wasn't able to accept and respond to his strong and compassionate feelings for her, Antonio's intensity made her uncomfortable: a stranger to love and harmony, at times, she preferred to reject him and forbid herself to share his belief of a better future for both of them.

Antonio found peace in Margarine's large bosom and would let himself go, sometimes sobbing into her buxom form. They often got together in the middle of the night, at the hour when the complex was getting ready to go to sleep. She'd become his source of inspiration, the one who listened to him attentively. Antonio would reveal his most extravagant longings and confide his most secret desires to her. He never criticized what she did with other men. As a matter of fact, he was careful to avoid the subject entirely. He loved her and was simply happy for the privileged moments they spent together.

Thanks to those tender moments in the basement, he was able to escape and find solace from the day-to-day burdens. Delicious, Margarine offered him a quick and peaceful journey toward ecstasy and respite with a gentle touch, the full plump expert lips toward his pelvic area. A conjugation of wounds and trials, they stole moments of quiet in their shared solitude amid the dust in the depth of block F. She gave him a maternal smile and caressed his slicked-down hair when he said:

—You know, Margarine, we should go away, both of us, far from here, just you and me, start all over again. You know, there are tons of places to visit in the world, and look at us, rotting here like rats. I'm going to take you away, you'll see ...

❧

Ever since they've known each other, Rosa Maria always takes the time to listen to her friend and console her in the face of disappointments. They share their dreams and their disillusions. Yet the feelings, the doubts, and the fears that paralyze Margarine when she thinks about Antonio, she's never found the words to express them.

Margarine earns money to have a good time every so often without having to calculate, let alone think about tomorrow. She suffers so much from missing him, she often confides to Rosa, her only friend since Antonio's passing. During the secret moments, Margarine loves to run her fingers through Rosa's black curls and all over her body in really slow, precise movements, in silence, tender moments stolen from sadness, a sort of nameless taboo relationship has nestled in between them over time.

A way to run away from the ghosts of her childhood, from the vague and painful memories. A man's footsteps heading toward the children's bedroom in the night, with the smell of alcohol and sweat. A cold little girl is trembling and tensing up in the depth of her soiled bed. Tears of incomprehension, yet the harm has already been done, and persists even today.

❧

—You see, Rosa, I don't even know anymore what happened ... but I think that was my first client!

❧

Margarine had told her about it on one of their first trips outside the projects, over by the grain fields, behind the country roads they took to get away, out of sight from all the prying eyes. The light, reflecting off the yellow fields, illuminated them both and extended as far as the naked eye could see on the plains of Île-de-France. Rosa and Margarine had taken off in a car borrowed from a guy in the neighborhood; its smoky and narrow interior was quickly filled with laughter and songs screamed at the top of their lungs, before parking at the edge of a forest. Stretched out in the cool shade of a tree, they opened up to each other and lost themselves in confidences. Rosa Maria allowed the light touches and slight kisses. It was a tacit agreement, let's not talk about it, I like it, but it's nothing, I'm not like that, it's Jason that I love, for life!

~

Rosa Maria gets down from the bench; she's getting ready to go.

—You'd be better off working like your sister, Rosa, instead of hanging around with that other sicko!

Margarine brings Rosa back to reality:

—Damn it, shit, it's way late, it's already dinnertime. I better go. My father's going to kill me, he won't miss the chance! All right, bye!

—Later, Rosa!

—Yeah, later.

Rosa Maria picks up the pace, bypasses a building, turns off the path, and crosses the lawn at the edge of the parking lot, before arriving at the entrance of the stairwell. She climbs the steps quickly up to the second floor. Out of breath, she knocks on the door. Worried, her sister Sonia opens up.

—Goddamn it, Rosa, you've got to be kidding. The old man's off the hook.

—I swear, Sonia, I really hurried!

—You're a pain in the ass. I'm completely wiped out from working at the cash register. I don't need your bullshit. Go on, go see him and apologize. Mom's with Anna in her room, she's afraid it's all going to get out of control!

But already Salvatore has moved toward his daughters, his eyes red with rage, his left fist clenched, his breath reeking of alcohol, mean, cursing, heavy, halting breathing, not open for discussion, belt wrapped around his right hand, malicious. He's ready to punish.

—Dad, I'm sorry, I didn't want to ...

An avalanche of slaps going in every which direction, the buckle of the belt launched at rapid speed by centrifugal strength, red marks then blue ones on Rosa's skin, her body contorted in vain attempts to get away. Rosa Maria cries, begs, she stumbles, staggers; her father grabs her by the arm, the painful pressure of a worker's hands, skin pincers gripping her muscles in. He hurls her against the wall, the deafening sound of a frail body crashing against the partition. Sonia dares to intervene:

—Stop, Dad, that's enough, she gets it.

Blind with rage, swarms of spittle spurting out of his mouth, beside himself, he screams:

—Oh, Sonia, get out of here, back off. Get out, otherwise … I'm going to teach her a lesson for constantly hanging out with those dirty Arabs and monkeys, as if there weren't enough French people around. She really needs to go looking elsewhere? Isn't it enough that her brother…

~

Terrorized, Sonia moves away from the direction of the leather belt that rises up before brutally striking Rosa Maria. Rosa Maria is in such a state of stupor that she's stopped crying. Her temples are burning, her mouth is bleeding a little bit, her head is buzzing horribly. She lies down, completely out of it on the floor to the entrance.

—What are we going to do with you? You want to be a whore or what? If you keep going on like that, you're going to finish like Antonio! Why do you keep hanging out with these darkies? You in heat or what?

Rosa Maria has gotten used to it over time and learned the routine of the blows. She knows that at some point it'll all stop, including the insults. She just has to escape into a dream, imagine herself elsewhere for a while, where everything is calm and beautiful, in a welcoming unspoiled nature surrounded by the music of birds singing.

Violent words are ephemeral, it'll all pass. Her greatest suffering is her love for Jason, a throbbing pain, a huge chunk right in the middle of her heart, an unbearable longing. Waiting? Punishment! His indifference? Torture! Where is he at this very moment, what is he doing? When will he recognize her love? She suppresses a sob, gathers her thoughts, to forget as quickly as she can, to run away from all the horrors, each time farther away. If Antonio were still here, he would protect her. So she imagines Jason, drop-dead gorgeous, pulling her toward him, bringing her close to him in one suave move that he alone knows how to pull off; they spin around like in an old-fashioned waltz, and it ends with him holding her tightly in his arms!

～

Holding her head in her hands, Sonia shakes it, empty, remorse for the helplessness, the constant affliction, forever latching onto them, hopeless. She cries.

Salvatore screams, hysterical, puffing, a purplish vein swells, pulsating intensely on the top of his head in the middle of his salt-and-pepper short-cropped hair.

—What are we gonna do with you, Rosa?

Anna, the youngest, comes running out of her mother's bedroom crying:

—You're cruel, you're going to kill Rosa!

A firm slap with the back of the hand stops the ten-year-old little girl dead in her tracks, and she runs through the corridor, screaming louder than before, right back to her room.

—Oh, enough of this goddamn racket! You're gonna shut your mouths, or else all hell's gonna break loose in that dago household of yours!

Exasperated, the neighbor on the third floor bangs on the floor before screaming in the stairwell. Drunk with rage, Salvatore replies:

—Fuck you, let's see if you got some real balls or not. Why don't you go *fa enculo* like your wife with all those Arabs when you're at your shit factory?

—Asshole, at least I have a job, jerk-off!

Amid the confusion of anger and insults, Rosa Maria slowly gets up. With her bruised body, she goes back to her room, undresses carefully to ease some of the suffering, and manages to slip into her nightgown before sliding under the covers.

The pain and the memory of the brutality wear off, music slowly takes over, silhouettes in graceful moves, she dreams. Beams of light, colorful fairy-like images, a party for Jason and her intertwined at the top of a hill bathing in sunlight. In their Sunday best, families admire them from down below, hugging and kissing, smiling. Even the neighbor is there to toast to their health with Salvatore.

Rosa Maria recalls the vacation in Sicily. Her father watches to be sure that she and her sisters do not go alone into the village to spare them the disgrace. He is kind, attentive, and protective. There is no stopover during the journey from Paris to Turin, the excitement of going, the enthusiasm in Salvatore's eyes, he sings, and everyone joins in at the top of their lungs, kisses on Angelina's cheeks, who's in a good mood, the car packed with gifts for the family, the break in open air, the Italian smells and sky.

Much later, the boat to Sicily, the local specialties, the mini pizzas, the balls of rice with tomato sauce, a foretaste of the country, the best moment of the trip.

Once they finally arrive at Aunt Graziella's house, freshness, calm, rest, the aromas of cooking and delights of the pots, a universe of ancient stones. Without waiting, first her father is going to go meet up with the men gathered at the port by the fish market, then he will spend the greater part of the day at his mother's place. Antonio is stretched out on a lounge chair in the garden, splendid with his white shirt wide open showing his muscular chest. He squints his eyes to protect himself from the bright sunlight, the head of the Native American shining on his belly. Her big brother is even more seductive in his younger sister's memories, an icon of purity to whom she attributes the qualities of an angel.

～

The burning sensation of the blows on her skin begin to temper. Rosa Maria rediscovers the scorching heat of the unspoiled island, not a building on the horizon and no interstate highways, a succession of little villages scattered all about in nature at the foot of the mountains, exuberant flora in the squelching heat, sand, few trees, palm trees, a strange and unique landscape. Sicily, that other world, Rosa Maria's blue skies. She sees herself again as a kid walking barefoot on the black lava stones of the pavements and roads, the dazzling light reflected by the white of the houses, the high temperatures that compel you to live at a slower pace and to fully experience each pore of the skin.

A hamlet on the hillside and in the plains, loving faces of friends from the hood, Rosa Maria is beautiful on Jason's arm. He is dressed in an elegant light blue linen shirt that allows a glimpse of the beautiful contours of his torso. Margarine embraces her and kisses her on the lips, Mouloud congratulates his beloved, Rosa smiles, happy to be finally basking in harmony ... She falls asleep.

Sunday goes by smoothly in the modest apartment. Salvatore is smoking, leaning on the windowsill, looking on with a blank stare at the building in front that obstructs his view, a block of cement inlayed with glass squares. He imagines the faces and lives of all the unknown people he's walked past practically every day over the years with indifference. The family man lives in exile, absent, with nowhere to turn and nothing to hope for, ever since the prospect of returning to the triumphal summers on his native island has come to an impasse with protracted unemployment. He applies himself with each mouthful of tobacco and nicotine he inhales; first the cheeks become hollow when the tips of the lips firmly pinch the tip of the filter, then the burning sensation invades his mouth and his throat before spreading into his lungs. A loner, Salvatore treats himself to these tiny scraps of ephemeral pleasures.

A couple of feet further down in the kitchen, Angelina is preparing lunch while humming a lullaby. She's managed to create a bubble in which she can appreciate the calm of the moment after the storm of the previous night and just allow herself to relax.

Her daughters, still in their nightgowns, are piled onto the sofa in front of the television, laughing every so often while watching their favorite show. They're not thinking about anything, content and carefree. In the living room, on the big commode, there is a black-and-white photo of their parents on their wedding day and a print of the three sisters. The portrait of the older brother has disappeared. As a matter of fact, the door to his bedroom is always locked. Angelina still can't bring herself to move one item in there. The very idea of it breaks her heart. It would be like suffering his death a second time. Hard to believe that in the past, the five-room apartment, bathroom, and separate toilet had completely impressed the couple newly arrived from Italy ready for a brilliant future.

⁓

Some days, Sonia, Rosa Maria, and Anna suffocate in their room that's become too small for them over the years, especially when the family atmosphere is so tumultuous. They feel like they're truly living in hell, one on top of the other with very little space and privacy. But once the timbre of the voices calms down, the tense foreheads relax, smiles return, and, within the four walls of the tiny room, a refuge is restored, the kingdom in which confidences and anxieties are shared, a secret garden, inaccessible to their parents, where Salvatore would never venture.

⁓

Their father wears a gray, exhausted mask, his eyes are dull, his back hunched. He watches the comings and goings of every passerby in the path delineated by weeds, which tremble feverishly following the whim of the fall breeze. The flowers that used to line it have long since withered from poverty, neglect, and acts of vandalism.

Antonio's ghost is omnipresent in Salvatore's daily life and otherwise in the Milano family's life; he has sealed their mouths in the unspoken, a bitter presence hovering in Rosa Maria's sadness, a reproach that weighs heavily on Salvatore's shoulders, a thorn in the most tender part of Antonio's grieving mother's heart. An indescribable chagrin consumes her like venom, inconsolable. His memory haunts her every single night and every morning again from the moment she opens her eyes, she worries about whether he has already woken up . . .

Salvatore forbids himself to cry for the loss of his son. He tries in vain to fight the profound grief buried in his soul and his flesh.

Happy images of Antonio playing on his knees haunt him, the remorse, the torture, years lost in misunderstandings with this son, so different. His absence affects Salvatore's brain, already fragile from the economic hardship, the silence, the lack of affection, time that keeps going by and resolving nothing, his daughters who avoid him and especially the disapproval in their eyes. Isolated, Salvatore is coming undone.

~

His gaze often lingers on this young blond girl, high heels and short skirt with long legs. He undresses her. Salvatore already knows her by heart, the way her rear end bounces with each step. He's lost in the bright red lipstick on her mouth; the subtle movement of her breasts beneath her provocative clothes sets off a flood of warmth in his chest. She makes him want to kiss her and even more, bite her, spread some warmth, some tenderness, gently caress her skin, smile, enjoy good feelings. She goes by. He watches the movement of her shapely figure, provocative, a dream of tender flesh; he pictures the velvety touch of a finger running all over his worn body, a longing, an obsession. He's possessed by Margarine, his desire for her breathes life back into him. When Salvatore is contemplating her, he forgets his patriarchal role, the intransigence, the inflexibility, and ventures toward gentleness. With her, everything is so simple. He sees himself nestling in with his swaying gait, his arm delicately holding her around the waist. His stern mask of days of misery is replaced with a radiating smile, she turns toward him and hugs him too. They walk, hand in hand, talking to each other in whispers right until she turns the corner and disappears behind the building. Salvatore comes back to reality and lights a cigarette.

Wilfried N'Sondé

For Angelina, the monotonous litany of each passing day begins on Monday morning. She wakes up at the crack of dawn, prepares breakfast for the whole family, and takes care of Anna, the baby, before heading off to work. Once she's quickly and carefully prepared herself, she transforms into a rapid shadow who leaves the building, always in a jog trot, and takes off into the street still covered in darkness.

The broken door in the hallway on the other side squeaks while opening. Another silhouette emerges in the beam of light coming from the streetlamp, exits, and feet hit the asphalt. Little by little, a crowd mainly of women huddle under the bus stop shelter. No one pays attention anymore to the giant advertisement that covers the back of the shelter, a superb-looking woman dark-complexioned on a sunny beach on the other side of the world, in a discreet bathing suit, toned body, smiling, black hair and generous hips, above her, the inscription reads: *Indulge yourself, Get away, Discover Bora-Bora!*

～

Then come the young mothers with dark circles of fatigue under their eyes. They hurry out into the first light of dawn behind their strollers, always running late, lagging behind, pushing tiny little humans, not yet sure of their footing, snot dripping from their noses, teary eyed, with the remains of a quickly eaten breakfast on their cheeks, tiny traces of jam and bread stuck to the corners of their mouths. The drowsy expression of children who've had too little sleep and are still catching up on some on their way to the daycare center. With hardly enough time to make themselves beautiful, the young mothers' heads are already filled with an interminable list of things to do that time will not allow them to accomplish, an inventory of criticisms from their unsympathetic employers and demanding, nagging spouses. Hours wasted handling administrative concerns. They've started a new week. These courageous young mothers will wait for Saturday, Sunday, to come up for air before the week starts all over again.

⌒

When the sun makes its way through the dark clouds, heads down, a slow belabored pace on the asphalt, the old, the retired, the forgotten await the unlikely visit of a family member. Memories to keep them going as long as their memory doesn't begin to fade. Loneliness.

⌒

Among them Lucien Marchand, wife deceased too soon, no children. Following a youthful existence filled with travel and adventures, life had crushed him to the point of making a human wreck of him. The image of his defeat has colored his face gray, sapped by cheap red wine and dark tobacco. He only leaves his apartment to head to the discount supermarket where, forever in a foul mood, he babbles nasty remarks with an evil eye. He buys the cheapest alcohol and stuffs it into his worn-out shopping bag. At times, when he's standing at the cash register of the bar and tobacco shop buying his weekly lotto ticket, there's the hope of having a new lease on life. He goes back home to the walls yellowed by nicotine stains and the asphalt and just hunkers down till the next morning. The rest of the time he spends vegetating in front of the TV or standing by the window irritated, arguing with surprised passersby and scolding children playing at the foot of the building. Because he is so bitter, the laughter and games coming from the other side of the street at the end of the day, and especially on weekends and during school vacation, get on his nerves. They disturb his state of boredom, interfere with the rumination in his sadness, thinking about the only woman who ever loved him. Lucien Marchand spews out all his frustrations, insults and foul language are always on the tip of his tongue, pointing his menacing finger at ten-year-old kids who get a kick out of really giving him a hard time. They then go off for a while and start up the mischief even louder than before. The sixty-something-year-old is on the verge of imploding; the medication he's on is no longer enough to calm his nerves.

—

Beneath the shed, as soon as the bus arrives, Angelina and the others pile on in without a single word, the sound of the engine is going, the click-clack of the stamped tickets paces the takeoff, no one looks at each other, everybody's heading to work with no visible joy or motivation. Angelina, she's happy to be making her way toward a new experience.

After several weeks of training, the municipality offered her a job as a cleaning lady. Rosa Maria's mother was very nervous about the prospect of having to return to school; her education had ended thirty years ago with a basic leaving certificate, after eighth grade. She was quick to remind herself that most of the other women didn't know how to read or write. Luckily, the skills required to do surface cleaning were basically learned on the job; you just had to repeat the same gestures over and over and progressively improve on your effectiveness.

Now she's earning a living for the first time and getting a taste, however feebly, of her independence and freedom. Even though she still loves and respects her husband, it's a relief to be spared the company of his unbearable silence in the back of the kitchen. Their best years together are now a distant memory.

She can still picture Salvatore, young, handsome, and as cool as a cucumber, singing her a serenade in his husky voice with his little wooden guitar, making eyes at her and extending a bouquet of wildflowers, blushing like a little boy. They got engaged in secret after an intense first kiss on the lips under an olive tree. He'd then taken her by the hand and, following tradition, taken her away for three days. Seventy-two hours of pure happiness for Angelina. Salvatore was attentive to her every last wish. He wove necklaces of rose petals, whispered sweet words in her ear, and kneeled down before her to pray to the Virgin Mary to give their love a chance. Tears in his eyes, he kissed her fingers, placed them on his cheeks, and drenched them in his tears. They subsequently resurfaced before her father to ask for her hand in marriage.

At the beginning, they loved each other like kids, intensely, and were married in no time. For the occasion, one of Angelina's sisters loaned her a white dress, the couple, much like the rest of the island, were seriously short on funds. The young bride must have only been about a couple of weeks' pregnant when Salvatore accepted the position in the automobile factory somewhere in the Paris area. The employer offered them a huge brand-new apartment in one of the public housing complexes with all the modern conveniences, toilet, bathroom, running water, and gas, reserved parking spots, playgrounds for the kids, and schools. It had all been conceived for six thousand families of workers, constructed with modern material made to last, steel, reinforced concrete, and asphalt. Salvatore and Angelina were amazed by the architecture of simple efficient geometric shapes, especially squares and rectangles, no blind spots, to prevent surprises, nothing had been left to chance. Angelina felt confident, she was overwhelmed with joy, and respect and admiration for Salvatore, who was himself proud to be able to offer his beautiful wife the kind of dignified life a lady deserves and a future for the children to come. They were among the first to move into the neighborhood.

❧

Nowadays, the late afternoons of the former Prince Charming are wiled away at a local bar until he heads on home to the evening meal prepared by his wife, all that's left of a family life that no longer resembles what they had both dreamed of. Salvatore is worn out, his voice is wedged in his throat with his suffering. He no longer understands anything about the life he leads, and his self-esteem is definitively gone, disappeared into a life of living off childcare benefits and the meager salaries of Angelina and his oldest daughter.

Angelina has let go, she's no longer looking to rediscover the man who used to hold her in his arms or surprise her over by the stove on his return from the factory, a kiss on the neck, electric tingling sensations going up and down her spine, the small of her back curving beneath the wave of desire, even if while smiling she would wiggle out from under his embrace and send him to go get ready for dinner.

She hardly recognizes him when he drags himself about and wanders around in the apartment, his aimlessness always taking him back to the kitchen window.

He smokes nonstop and only goes out at the end of the day to head over to the counter to drink, never speaking to anyone. Within an hour and a half, he's back home even more morose than before he left.

~

Thanks to her job, Angelina is able to get out of the oppressive closed-off universe in which her relationship is trapped. She has made friends with her new colleagues, women whose biographies resemble her very own. They share their joys and take each other in their arms to lament. They're on their way to emancipation. Ever since the conjugal bed went cold, this lone housewife and mother has reconnected with her body and dreams of having two twin beds in the room, but they're in desperate need of money. Angelina is relieved, the girls have grown up, even Anna, the youngest, has outgrown her bras and her skirts. She's so adorable. Courageous, Sonia is working at the supermarket; the poor girl had to sacrifice her studies by quitting high school to get a real job, too bad, but they needed the extra income.

As for Rosa, who has always been secretive, she's gotten worse since her brother's death. Angelina's son had been such an adorable, playful baby, always laughing, so sensitive, too refined for his father. Antonio had made for a lot of problems as a teenager, constantly criticizing and wanting to change the world. Like the time he organized a demonstration in front of the police station with the young people in the neighborhood to protest against police violence and racial profiling. But Antonio also managed to get some space down at the local youth center to volunteer as an academic tutor.

A few months before his death, he had changed big-time; he no longer slept at home and would even disappear from the neighborhood for several days at a time. One night, Salvatore had brought him back home from the police station before giving him a thorough beating. Antonio never did come back home after that, except to steal. He lost a lot of weight, looked terrible, and sometimes even came by at her workplace to ask for money . . . Angelina didn't recognize him anymore. He frightened her. Then came the tragic end, the shock, the horror, the mystery because no one knows exactly what happened.

A mother never forgets the day she has to bury her first child.

ON THAT AFTERNOON, groups had gathered over time in front of the hallway entrance; facial expressions were grave, closed off, heads lowered, bodies stiff and stoic. The complex was at half-mast, preparing the journey to the final destination of one of its own, the atmosphere was heavy. Rain threatened to pour down. Girls and women were holding back tears, huge knots of sadness contracted under their eyelids. They were moving their heads back and forth, slowly, in silence, eyes red and lifeless. Everybody was turning on their heels like zombies, hands in the pockets of the pants they wore for special occasions, impatient, overwhelmed by what had happened. The elderly had dug up funeral outfits that had been buried in the back of the closet up till this point. The tasteless display of clothing of somber colors, black, gray, from another era, a truly peculiar tableau next to the getups the friends of the deceased had improvised that morning, dressed in their everyday wear except for a large piece of black cloth wrapped around the arm. For most of them, this was their first funeral. The bitterness ran deep, the anger too, still anesthetized from the immense shock of the news. Antonio, deceased only a few days prior, had had a unique role in the neighborhood, he was everybody's friend, the big brother, the one who made everyone feel proud, even courageous, and who gave everyone a lot of attention and affection. A caring hand on the shoulder, with his enthusiasm and convictions, he managed to convince people they would come out OK at the other end. It was about taking a stand and taking action together.

The procession waited for the family to arrive before beginning the walk to the cemetery. No one had the courage to look up at the window on the second floor where Salvatore had stationed himself as usual to observe and smoke cigarettes. Stone-faced, he ignored the crowd, his resolve could not be stirred, a cold expression despite his wife's pleas, there was no way he was going to be accompanying his son to his grave. Inconsolable, her face hidden beneath a veil of black lace, Angelina wound up joining, however painfully, the head of the procession. She had cried so much that she almost collapsed with each step she took. Her eldest daughter, Sonia, held her up by the arm. Her other two children followed behind, hand in hand.

The hearse opened the procession by moving to the pace of those walking; the column of people advanced slowly beneath the drizzle, trickles of cold water, beating on their faces. A cruel wind kept blowing stronger and stronger, letting the first brown leaves of the fall dance a macabre ballet in the air. The dull, clammy sky punctured the menacing clouds. The whole neighborhood was mourning Antonio. A curtain of grayness spread throughout the alleyways and paths, engulfing the inside of buildings, descending into the basements, and covering all the cement and asphalt. It was an unbearable farewell; legs dragged along heavily. The crowd went past the football field and veered left toward the junction, passing beneath the sad expressions hiding behind the curtains of each window in the complex. They then made their way on to the right beyond the gas station. The funeral procession continued straight ahead toward the railway station and, just before the roundabout, turned again to the left to reach the cemetery on the edge of the old city. The beautiful gray roofing and cream-colored facades of the suburban homes were already discernable.

Sitting at the wheel of an unmarked police vehicle in front of the annex to the mayor's office, Police Commissioner Jacques Bridin observed the procession. For him, the situation could potentially explode. The mysterious demise of Antonio Milano, pseudo-political agitator, troublemaker, occasional drug dealer, completely idolized, especially among the ranks of the young people in a problem area like project 6000, could easily exacerbate the tensions between the community and law enforcement.

Wilfried N'Sondé

Family and friends finally gathered before the priest, standing close to the mother, who was in tears, and the sisters, who were choking in their sobbing, their eyes riveted to the coffin and the gaping hole, ready to welcome Antonio Milano, the beloved brother of Rosa Maria. In the distance, the bad weather rumbled and at times drowned out the moaning in the congregation and the words of the clergyman. Unshakeable in his litany, he evoked the ravages of drugs, a plague of modern times, so young a life called back to the Almighty Lord. He made an appeal for calm so that the soul of the deceased could rest in peace. It was important to continue to have faith.

When it was over, everyone took turns embracing Angelina and her three daughters, expressions of sorrow, lips murmuring condolences following the embraces. Then the crowd dispersed peacefully, everybody was looking for shelter, the downpour had intensified. It was the most sordid day in Angelina's life.

❧

Wearing a veil, Angelina hurried into the rising dawn and the drizzle of October, amid the headlights of cars decorating the city with strange garlands of yellow, white, and red. The cacophonic symphony of shoes on the asphalt sounded the rhythm of the weekday mornings. The huge colorless concrete bars poured out a crowd making headway in a hurry. Dressed from head to toe in sadness, Angelina rushed in the direction of the train station, where trains were waiting to head for the capital and the bus she needed to take was standing ready to transport her to her workplace.

Day breaks, and out of the buildings pours a noisy population of school kids, dressed in the latest fashion, colors, and extravagances, still sporting smiles on their faces, unwavering enthusiasm:

—How's it going, Rosa, everything cool?

—Yeah, and you?

Four kisses to greet each other, everyone's talking about the latest news in the hood and the party at Black Move.

—Saturday was the shit at Black Move, wasn't it, Rosa?

—Oh yeah, great! Patrick really tore it up with the sound system, I swear!

—On my mother's life, Rosa, he really tore the shit up. By the way, why did you get into it with Fatou?

—I dunno ... I didn't even really understand ... She dances really good, you know, so I was looking at her, and she didn't like that at all ... I really don't know, I don't even know the girl!

—I dunno, but she is slammin', damn! Right, Rosa, I'm gonna be late, better not miss the bus, gotta push off, later.

Rosa Maria's school week begins with a ballet of bad grades, the joy of meeting up with her friends again, being summoned to the principal's office: who trashed the English teacher's car? Fire extinguisher thrown from the third floor a few feet away from the principal, sick leave for several weeks, nervous breakdown, teaching staff goes on strike with no intention of giving in to intimidation, opening of a computer room with internet access much to the delight of the students, sending home the troublemakers, destruction of classroom material, peddling soft drugs right at the school entrance ... Sharing the giggles with friends during break time, sharing cigarettes on the bench in the back of the schoolyard, winks and stolen kisses beneath the poplar trees, some kids trying to remake the world are caught up in a heated discussion, others are struggling alone, misunderstood in the twists and turns of adolescence ...

The site of Rosa's general high school education consists in two dark green buildings on the outskirts of the city, boxed in between the highway and a forest in the vicinity of the industrial zone. Two rectangular structures built in a style that no art history book would even bother to comment on. The buildings had been put up in haste; there'd been no time to waste. A black metal wire fencing of nearly five feet frames the enclosure. In front, the bicycle shed, a real cemetery of stripped bicycles, wheels, frames, bikes abandoned by their owners after having been vandalized or the object of vengeance. In the middle, a concrete courtyard much like all the others and, in the back, sports fields with their nets and baskets torn, within the first months of having been inaugurated in the presence of the mayor and the deputy for the electoral district. Since then, every morning a noisy crowd makes its way there, full of excitement and hope in spite of the difficulties and the bad reputation of the school.

~

Rosa Maria is bored during school hours. She no longer understands the classes and couldn't care less. Her nose stuck to the window, her gaze is lost beyond the sinister picture of the neighborhood, spiked with tall dirty bars for buildings, a depressing maze, and below cars in the parking lots.

She imagines golden-hued landscapes, birds flying high above, radiant sunlight on the wheat fields, on the frost or on the dark ground, the dance of pollen in April, the perfumes from the powder of the wheat come harvest time. Her daydreaming drifts further following the vibrant variations of colors according to the seasons, gold when the plain burns in the summer, the brown of the leaves and the black of the sticky ground that seal the autumn and winter, the green flowering of the spring, beneath a gray or blue sky. Further along, another world, the unknown, travels. The high school student concocts well-positioned trees lining the roadside, exciting cities that are great to live in, all kinds of colors. She imagines rivers where boats sail, luxury cruise liners heading for the end of the world. That's where she should have lived, that way, Antonio wouldn't have had to die the way he did on the pavement behind the supermarket. Rosa Maria is taking flight from her world, the reality of her life is oppressive, she's made a little hole so that light can come in amid the gloom, and she's immersed herself in it. Another dimension, a mirage, where her brother is still alive and Jason is madly in love with her.

An insolent student, unruly, closed off to even her most motivated teachers who have become the target of her profound feeling of malaise. A revolt is brewing deep within her and is trying to find the path that will take her far away, to sunny days, dreams of happiness, gold and blue.

Her teachers have failed in this remote unknown region of Île-de-France, flanked by a train station with a ridiculous name and lost to anonymity on the Parisian regional public transportation map. Their motivation has been severely tested. It's the kind of battle that is won or lost by wearing down one's opponent. It's about not giving up too soon while still holding on to your sanity. They're struggling to keep their passion for the subject they teach alive in the face of a mistrustful population with serious hang-ups, hiding behind defensive, impolite, and at times, even aggressive attitudes. Different groups have formed, and misunderstandings have come between the different generations. Everybody risks failure and discouragement. Disenchantment is lurking.

Rosa Maria is not at all concerned with the content of the school programs she suspects have been conceived most importantly for students who have nothing to do with her and her classmates. She is constantly feeling misjudged by her teachers, who seem distant and incapable of ever questioning the way they do things in an effort to try to understand her world. Rosa Maria is wasting her time at school and ruining the experience for the whole class, just like her brother did.

～

Wilfried N'Sondé

Antonio stopped going to high school during his senior year. He never felt like he fit in, felt looked down on. On principle, he took a stand as an enemy of the institution. He organized a strike that was widely supported by students and threatened to sequester the principal to protest against some racial epithets he was said to have uttered. The administration sent him home.

❧

High school life keeps on going with its attendant terror in the corridors, dreams for the future made and undone a thousand times during break time, rumors of sexual harassment in the girls' bathroom, for some, an enthusiasm for learning, a fierce desire to get through it, to climb the social ladder using their brains, fights in the entrance hall, some suspicious transactions behind the bus stop, the disciplinary board, the pride of obtaining a high school diploma with distinction. The weekend, to have some breathing room.

Boredom, anger, sadness, but also the pleasure of being together and exchanging ideas with friends pulls Rosa Maria limping along right until the bell rings at noon on Saturday.

Rosa Maria stops in front of tower C. The guys and girls from the neighborhood are arriving in clusters. They've been waiting for this moment for a week now, good mood, party outfits, brand-name clothing, sweat suits. Everybody remembers the success of the previous week. The reputation of Black Move, the good sound system, not a single fight, and a smoking ambience, word had traveled throughout the hood. Rosa Maria takes note with some real concern about the new faces showing up. She's especially paying attention to the teenage girls most likely to intensify the competition that's already so tough when it comes to getting Jason's attention.

A small mob gathers near the entrance to the basement, the crowd comes closer, surprised to find an unlikely couple wearing orange armbands with the inscription *Police* on their civilian clothes.

Captain Moussa Traoré and his partner, Lieutenant Laurence da Silva, are waiting. They've closed the door, posted a stop sign on a yellow fluorescent ribbon, prohibiting entry. The steps down to the party are closed off. Administrative decision.

The commissioner for the area has assigned two plainclothes officers to the neighborhood to work closely with the residents of project 6000 to better respond to their concerns.

—Hello, folks. I'm Captain Moussa Traoré from the national police force. This is my colleague, Lieutenant da Silva. No music today. The mayor along with police headquarters have decided to seal off the entrance to the basement for the peace of mind of the local residents, especially since nothing is up to safety standards for festive activities. It's also being closed off for your safety. You certainly didn't realize it, but it's toxic to stay down there for that many hours. The air quality is not good at all, and with the cigarettes, it's seriously dangerous! Why don't you go to the real clubs? Around here you're causing too much noise.

❧

Sure of his position, Moussa Traoré raises his hands, smiles, and adds:

—And don't worry, this is only temporary. I'm going to personally do all I can to fix this. The administrators in charge of community services are going to be asked to find activities for you that are safer and more appropriate. Proposals will be made to you shortly.

A voice rises up in the middle of the gathering:

—You're boring us shitless with your TV reporter attitude. Take your big fat head and clear out of here. We want to dance, that's all, we don't need you or your bullshit plans. No one lives in this building, so cut the spiel, we're not bothering anyone! You're not from around here, go on, move it!

Laurence da Silva can feel the tension rising. She'd given in to her superiors reluctantly. They hadn't left her much choice. She and Moussa were going to have to deal with the projects.

They have to keep things under control, especially since there are many more young people than they'd imagined. She takes Moussa aside:

—Captain, we can't back off, but we definitely have to defuse the situation. The young people are beginning to get agitated. There are only two of us; perhaps we should call for backup, you never know...

Moussa Traoré addresses the crowd:

—Calm down and keep it clean. Listen, we respect you, so please show the same respect; cooperate, and everything will be all right. We're aware that few activities were planned for the teenagers and young adults in this neighborhood; we're going to fix it.

—You're right, there's nothing for us, so we done what we could. We don't know you. We're just asking you to stop bothering us, to go back to the police station, this is our turf. You forgotten you're black or what? You didn't even bother to find out who took Antonio out, this nightclub was his idea, you may even be the one who bumped him off! Get lost, goddamn it, we want to dance. Now fuck off, we're gonna hit it for Antonio. Come on, guys, let's go!

~

The crowd moves slowly toward the two officers; the confrontation is close. Moussa maintains his position, his arms open. Overcome with fear, Laurence hesitates but stands right by her captain's side, calm, stolid.

~

The invective is infectious, an inexpressible clamor coming from the gathering is menacing, irritation, anger, the Black Move regulars are moaning and groaning, you can hear:

—Shit, motherfuckers, torch the place ... Racists! We're gonna max out the sound, up in your face ...

Fists tighten deep down in their pockets:

—Yeah, it's always the same, we don't have the right to anything, motherfuckers, we're not going to let you roll all over us!

~

Suddenly, someone from the building in front is chuckling, his voice covers up the racket when he lets out:

—This isn't Africa, go on and wreak havoc somewhere else. Go on, get lost, faster than that, go on, scram, shoo!

A man at the window, in a white undershirt, a thick, graying, overflowing head of hair with a vengeful evil eye, screams:

—Go, faster than that! Go bust your lazy ass fathers' balls, get out of here, scram!

Lucien Marchand, former corporal in the colonial army, embittered from his best years in the service of the nation spent beneath the tropics, watches the scene. Still proud for having brought civilization to the savages with swift kicks in the behind. After twenty years in uniform, he solemnly asserts as one might conclude after much deliberation:

—The Muslim is deceitful, the Negro is lazy!

Looking down from his third-floor apartment, he regrets watching his country go adrift. It's killing him to see that the land for which he sacrificed his youth and shed blood is sinking into complete chaos, noise, and filth. It's no longer our home!

A misanthrope, Lucien Marchand has been living alone since his wife passed away from a devastating cancer. Helpless, he witnessed the agony of the one person in whom he could truly believe. No doctor could save her from this treacherous illness, which gnawed at her from the inside. He tried everything, knocked at every single door, and no luck. The indifference to their distress further isolated them. She died in his arms, on her side of their bed. Lucien kept vigil over her body for a whole night, shedding lots of tears before calling for help.

His wife, his final link to the world ... Nowadays, hours, sometimes whole days, go by without him ever saying a word to anyone.

Exasperated, he can't take it anymore. Everybody's doing whatever the hell he or she wants at the foot of the building. Insecurity. He finds all these foreign languages in the street intolerable, daily aggression to his ears, the swarm of impolite, dirty, rowdy kids, an invasion especially during vacation time, from morning till night, sometimes late into the night. Torture. The backfiring of scooters and all the other motorized engines. No, they don't respect anything or anybody, these people, wild animals, not to mention all those illegal immigrants who don't even speak French. Having lodged numerous complaints and written letters to the mayor and commissioner, he sees the authorities have finally taken action to stop the deafening mayhem on Saturday afternoons.

—Get going, you little shits, go back home, go back to your countries where you belong. I don't wanna see you round here anymore!

Serious rage rises up in his direction, a flood of threats, the excitement of the young people is turning to hate:

—Shut your ass, you son of a bitch. What, you bored now? You ain't got your wife to bang around no more? You've been on our case ever since she kicked it. Get the fuck outta here or you'll regret it.

—Bunch of idiots, you don't have the right to talk about her, you better shut your traps ... Don't you ever!

In the middle of the irritated crowd, Jason stamps his foot firmly on the ground several times:

—Fucking shit, sick and tired of this shit, man. They're always fucking after us!

◦

After a long week of organizing all types of articles on shelves under the authority of his unpleasant boss, taking out the trash, and cleaning the floor of the minimarket where he works, the young man has focused all his free time on the Saturday afternoon party. Besides his job, his energy goes into making preparations.

He finishes his beer in one final gulp and wipes his mouth with the back of his hand. An unsavory determination is beaming from his gaze. He's wearing his black well-polished shoes, his white jeans, and a light blue polo under a light coat. This morning, he stopped by at Boubacar's, the hairdresser. He's got class, style. He's ready to dance and do his show; the police are robbing him of his show. It's too much! And that other racist is laying it on way too thick:

—Get lost, I'm telling you. What are you waiting for? Are you deaf or what, you don't understand French?

—No, now you're going way too far. We're not going to let you treat us like this, shit!

Rosa Maria edges her way next to Jason. She finds him so handsome, drop-dead gorgeous. She whispers in his ear:

—It's not a big deal, Jason, maybe they'll open up next week. Come on, things could get out of hand here, everybody's getting irritated. Don't listen to the old fart, don't pay attention to what he's saying, he's always mean, this guy. Let it go, please!

The young man's hard of hearing, beside himself, always the same injustice, humiliation nonstop. He works five days a week and earns a miserable income. It's only during the festivities in the basement that Jason exists fully, the uncontested king, the looks the girls beam his way when they fall on him tearing it up in the basement. He snaps:

—They're all pissing me off!

Suddenly, he insults the neighbor's mother; the others follow up, echoing him, invective erupts from the crowd:

—Go home to your mother, that whore, stick a pen or whatever you want deep into . . .

Wilfried N'Sondé

Captain Moussa Traoré is worried and calls for calm:

—Hey, hey, it's OK, let's calm down! Sir, please. Close your window, don't aggravate the situation!

Things risk escalating. A bottle of beer is thrown into the air, flies a moment in the open air, and winds up smashing Lucien Marchand right in the face, already reddened and distorted by anger. He screams, the cry of a wounded animal drowned out in the fever coming from the street, and disappears from the rectangular window frame.

The police go into a tailspin:

—My God, who did that?

Everybody's still laughing when the former soldier reappears at the dormer window, his face scarlet from blood and rage, with a hunting rifle in his hand. He points it and mumbles vengeful words:

—Bastards, little shits, I am going to take care of you, you bunch of dirty Arabs and Negroes. I'm going to smoke the whole lot of you!

He points the gun. A horrible detonation rips through the sky of project 6000. Another shot follows. Screams, tears, an all-out stampede, scrambling, making a run for it. Moussa Traoré and Laurence da Silva, horrified, make big gestures with their arms and urge the young people to take shelter. An SOS call is launched by telephone. We need backup urgently. Maximum state of alert.

IN THE CONFUSION of trying to get away, Rosa Maria hangs on to Jason's hand. He drags her into the maze of the complex. Along with others, they cross the square in front of the shopping center, in an all-out race to survive, widespread panic, desperation, screaming, some crying.

Jason and Rosa stop behind the supermarket. She's pale, and her whole body is shaking from the chills. He tries his best to console her.

—Calm down now, we're out of danger. We're going to go hang out at my aunt's place. She lives opposite here and is still on vacation.

—Jason, what's happened is horrible. I'm afraid, I have a bad feeling about this. This is where they found my brother, we better go somewhere else.

—Don't worry, we're going to leave.

He smiles tenderly and holds her close to him, kisses her furtively on her forehead, and takes her with him:

—Come, Rosa, we're going to go get some air.

Once they arrive at the apartment, calm and secure, their veins still pounding with adrenaline, wide-eyed and in a state of stupor, they collapse onto the sofa. Dumbfounded, their gazes cross in the middle of the modest living room.

A big chandelier of false crystal weighs down the ceiling above, below it is unusual and tacky furniture. There are synthetic rugs on the floor to mask the holes and wear and tear of the old carpeting. A prayer stool has pride of place to the right of the television, and on the left side, a dusty Bible lies on the commode. The painted wallpaper is dull and peeling in places. On the wall, the annual calendar of the Parisian firemen is hanging by a nail. Next to it on the furniture made of plywood, the photo of two toothless little girls and a boy a little bit older, his face branded with a false smile. A sad universe, with no fantasy.

Distraught, Rosa Maria and Jason watch each other, the movement of their chests slowly calm down, and they regain their breath. A stirring is rising in the air.

—Holy shit, I can't believe it ... What a mess, shit, I shouldn't have ...

He heads toward the window to assess the situation.

—Holy shit, it's complete panic out there. I think there's gonna be trouble tonight ...

—Can I have a glass of water, Jason?

Jason goes into the kitchen and returns with a carafe in his hand. He serves her and sits down.

—Shit, it's all my fault, I shouldn't have thrown that bottle. I dunno what came over me, holy shit ...

Worried, Jason runs his hand over the top of his head several times. Rosa Maria slides over next to him.

—It's OK, Jason, you didn't mean to hurt him. You were angry, that's all, it happens to everybody, and plus I don't think the policemen know that it was you. Gotta calm down now, relax!

~

She caresses his forehead. Rosa Maria's body temperature is rising. Jason is certainly present, so close. This is her chance. Her temples redden, a flow of saliva in her mouth, her pupils dilate, the palms of her hands wet, butterflies in her stomach. She moves closer to Jason, lost in his thoughts, gets up, lays her head on his torso, her eyelids close, she puts her arms around him and breathes more and more intensely. Rosa Maria is losing herself in the rhythm gathering momentum in her chest. The sweet smell of the young girl clings to Jason. Surprised by the desire that suddenly overcomes him, instinctively, he begins to caress her black curls.

—Hey, Rosa, what's going on with you?

Rosa Maria places her mouth on his, let's herself go. Her head spins a little, she sees light, the Sicilian light, the heat of summers, the scorching heat on the skin makes the heart gallop. She holds her lover even tighter, just enough to be able to feel his body pressing on hers as though he wants to melt into her. Rosa Maria smiles and exhales slowly, then she raises her head up gently, the dream has found its place in her arms, she's tasting it. In one breath she can barely contain, her lips give way to:

—You know, Jason ... I love you ... Since forever, you know when you first arrived from your country, you kept saying how it was always hot there, you seemed sad, I immediately fell for you! I think about you day and night. I dream about you, you know ... it hurts me.

Without really listening to Rosa but already feeling excited, Jason kisses her with a passionate intensity, tongues intertwine and suck each other, his hands quickly make their way under the young girl's baggy clothing and discover her subtle curves. Lacking in a loving caress, his fingers press and slide on her moist skin. Jason quickly undresses her and discovers the underwear of a little girl.

—I love you, I love you!

Rosa Maria whispers this to him once his mouth has liberated hers before enveloping a breast. Jason removes her bra and panties. Rosa Maria is now completely naked. Drunk, she offers him her slender late-adolescent body whose femininity is slowly surfacing. Convulsive movements traverse her shoulders, her belly, and her thighs. She closes her eyes. Jason lets his pants fall to his ankle, he undresses quickly by hopping out of them and then lays Rosa Maria on the sofa. He opens her legs and takes her forcibly. She shivers, her fingers tense, and she plants her nails into his back. Rosa Maria moans and bites her lip. The pain stings and burns her intimate parts, but she endures it, because the miracle is inside her!

Jason embraces her roughly, groans with pleasure, sweats, and brings her more intensely toward him. Rosa Maria screams her love. The hot abrupt tide comes and goes, then everything rises up right in her chest, a wave that sublimates the carnal tear. She finally remembers the taste of happiness, cries, laughs, her eyes travel far away, head toward Italy, to the region of Naples that continues on to Sicily, to the left, the sunny cliffs, below to the right, the immensity of the blue sea of incomparable beauty, images from her childhood that convinced her a long time ago that God really exists.

She closes her eyelids, glides above the island overwhelmed by sunlight, and rushes into the narrow strip of land between the church and the Mediterranean Sea. Antonio is stretched out on the sand, his elbows holding up his torso, his eyes behind dark sunglasses, looking on at the infinite blue, he is gorgeous in his black pants, short hair pulled back, barefoot. He only has eyes for his little sister, mischievous and joyful, splashing in the water.

So many images and memories revived as Jason sighs and comes inside of her. Majestic, she is the princess of the skies, her lover by her side. Rosa Maria radiates, sumptuous, adorned in the dress whose photo she had ripped out of a magazine in the dentist's office. A magnificent creation, flesh-colored dress in jersey and draped chiffon worked into layers and decorated with ruche. Jason loves her and is making her dance above the calm sea, zero gravity, far from the village and the hills. Their skin scintillates in beautiful layers of brown and milky white, together they break free.

Exhausted, empty, Jason lay on the timid curves, still panting, absent. Rosa Maria ignores the pain. These few minutes are like an eternity of completeness, a volley of intense and infinite sensations. Love between her lips for a few minutes and she has reconnected with azure, the beauty of the days, joy.

～

Coming back from ecstasy, Jason rises up and observes her, surprised, almost disappointed, as though he has just come down from a mirage. Once he is standing, he looks around him, gathers up his belongings, and starts to get dressed.

—Oh no, not that, goddamn it. Why didn't you say something, Rosa? We would have been careful! Look at this shit, you got blood everywhere, even on the carpet. Hey, wake up, shit, are you dreaming or what? Gotta clean up all of this area here before it dries, my aunt is super neurotic about sex, God, and all that shit. If there's a single trace at all when she comes home, she's going to kill me! Hey, Rosa, you hear me or what? You gotta get a move on it, hey, oh!

A torrid and sticky fever all over her skin, childhood lullabies fill her ears, Rosa Maria is nothing but sweetness, she's gliding, levitating, and taking off. She has distanced herself from the world, a satellite on a gentle, steady course, inaccessible, untouchable. She's holding on to her happiness and does not intend to let it go; pleasure has rooted itself deep within, well anchored in her belly. Rosa Maria's heart is racing. She opens her eyes and directs the incandescence of the sensations of the moment at Jason. The young man only understands that she's not able to grasp what he's saying. He goes off into the kitchen:

—Goddamn it, seriously, sometimes you are completely out of it, Rosa!

He comes back, a sponge and a bucket in his hand, and washes the bloodstains. While getting dressed, Rosa Maria takes in the last images of that long-awaited moment, making love with Jason. Once she is dressed, she quietly waits for him to finish cleaning. Jason finds her a bit stupid, the girl is starting to annoy him.

—What else do you want, Rosa?

—Do you want to kiss me?

—No, seriously, Rosa, that's it, you're starting to annoy me. We had a good time, you and me, you wanted it, me too, we did it nice and easy, that's it! Don't go imagining stuff like because we slept together, you're now my girlfriend or something like that! Plus, you gotta get out of here now. I got stuff to do, I have to go see what's going on outside, I don't wanna leave the guys all alone. Come on, bye, we'll catch up sometime, Rosa.

Rosa Maria opens the door and takes off. She heads down the stairs, ignoring the clamor mounting louder and louder. On her way home, she crosses some of the young people from the neighborhood, overexcited, the disturbances have started, the sounds of breakage are announcing a riot.

Wilfried N'Sondé

The young girl holds on ever so tightly to her daydreaming and looks up to the sky. Her circular gaze touches the horizon; there are gray buildings, the dark roofs, and way down in the bottom, the fervor of violence intensifies and is already burning on the empty lot, the waltz of police vehicles is blocking the national highway in a concert of sirens and cop lights. Pandemonium.

A COUPLE OF hours after the gunshots, project 6000 turns into chaos, a news item, screams, pain, panic ... Riot.

Bitterness invading hearts, anger intensifying in the corridors of the buildings and avenues of the neighborhood. Rage is brewing, disturbing, looks for a rhythm and finds destructive madness, longing to exist and change everything. It's accelerating. Sneakers hit the pavement, uneven thumps, mad rush. The asphalt is shaking up its sons. It has placed a metal bar in their brains. Hemoglobin is pumping and rushing to temples. Pockets of brutality are exploding in loud crashes. The damage is about to begin! With his fingers knotted up deep into the pockets of his synthetic sweatpants, Mouloud huffs and puffs between his clenched teeth:

—Tired of it, there's gonna be trouble, you're gonna see. Tonight, the shit's gonna hit the fan!

Blood and tears are going to flow in the streets, the vigor of young pissed-off boys, determined to take down everything in their path! Their mouths howl and become the mouths of wolves with jaws wide open, ready to bite. They empty the trash containers on the sidewalks, the collective hysteria is propelling them violently into the windows of supermarkets; some are being splashed with gasoline and then burned, a blaze, apocalyptic thunder, applause. The crowd dances while jumping in the air, a disturbing commotion rises up from within the heart of the concrete. Stones, aggressively thrown, crash against windshields.

The daily frustrations and despair have gotten into the pores of the skin, obstructing the neurons and wreaking havoc on the brain. Rage is brewing and transforming into hate. Anger explodes, bloodshot razor-sharp eyes like blades. This is the last straw, the resentment of the outcasts, forever the losers, it all spills over onto the asphalt.

Jason is also there, his gaze injected with fire. He makes his way through the crowd and uses his hands around his mouth to be heard. His voice travels far:

—Yeah, we're gonna unleash tonight, we don't give a damn, we've had enough! Shit's gonna go down, we're going to break everything!

The deafening noise of a tide rising dangerously, rolling, getting bigger, rushing, dressed as a storm, a devastating blow right into the main artery of the projects. A frightening, uncontrollable crowd. Mouths going astray in death threats, spewing obscenities, fueling each other in nervous laughter. In the chaos, the school and day care center have been trashed by groups of kids barely out of kindergarten. They were breastfed on concrete long before they even learned to walk. Feet and fists strike and wind up destroying the one bus shelter they have. The broken glass partially hides the ad with the woman still smiling. In the image on the ground, bare feet bathe in turquoise water. She is dressed in a discreet bathing suit that she wears low on her hips. Her brown skin is decorated with a necklace that barely hides her chest. Her hair is shining, flowing down in thick, full waves. Her smile inspires the women and men of project 6000 to dream of freedom and warmth; it's a mirage of escape that's been planted in the heart of the projects for all of them to see. Above her, an inscription in gold letters, in a dazzling blue sky. The advertisement lingers on the ground, a chimera for the poor, forgotten.

◆

Rage is still brewing, more and more intensely. A sinister temperature warms the atmosphere among all the rectangular towers, a disorderly movement fed by nerves on edge. Adolescent palms, firm and moist, brandish iron bars, shards of bottles, and stones. A convulsion in the air that unhinges the children and frightens the mothers barricaded in their homes. Fear knots their guts, powerless before the drama, they lose themselves in prayers and supplications, that it all comes to an end quickly, that the boys return home, why is there always tragedy? Their stubby fingers nervously twist the edges of aprons, anxiety, violence, all over again. The unbearable anguish of silence settling in, just before the huge shock. The vicious circle of chaos swells dangerously, spreading, fed by a deleterious feeling, sadness, a lot of misunderstanding, and the thirst for revenge.

—They're shooting at us like rabbits. No, we're not going to accept that, my word, tonight there's going to be shit!

Infuriated, they've come to claim their piece of the pie, reach for the zenith, beyond the misery, by breaking whatever they have to. Locked up in an enclosure of concrete towers like in a vault, the brain reaches the limit of implosion, an engine that gets carried away and winds up exploding. The overwhelming injustice in the maze of the neighborhood, racial profiling by police, vacation in front of the television, cheap, tasteless food, washed down with sodas of improbable colors. Bitterness slips into the parking lots, bursts onto the avenues, and screams justice for everyone! The heckling, a cacophony of profanity, threatening, because they're shooting at them like animals.

~

The backup requested by Captain Moussa Traoré took the maniac in for questioning. Once he'd returned from his moment of insanity, Lucien Marchand regretted terribly his action and turned himself in voluntarily to the police. Protected by the officers who came to arrest him in his home, the sexagenarian left his building in handcuffs, dazed, he rolled his wild eyes like a hangdog. He seemed to not have a clue about what was happening and was very frightened before the hostile crowd, insulting and threatening.

~

Overwhelmed by what was happening, Moussa and Laurence tried in vain to restore order and to reason with the young people, who persisted and blocked the road:

—We're staying right here. He's ours, we're going to skin him, we're gonna finish him! He shot at us like we were in a fair. We're gonna give him a dose of his own medicine! This time, we're not gonna let it slide, too bad for him, he came looking for it!

~

The tormented clamor of the growing number of adolescents forced the civil servants to take refuge in their van.

The young people kept a good distance. They hesitated before crossing the line. Rage was brewing but had yet to explode. Laurence feared the worst. She was not trained for this kind of scenario; there were no known procedures to follow. She watched Moussa, who was by now having a meltdown, his expression betrayed profound doubt, he no longer looked at all like the upright proud man who so often impressed her. The commotion was becoming oppressive and contrasted with the silence that reigned in the passenger compartment. The windows to the vehicle were up, the doors locked; the other police officers were preparing for conflict. Moussa fell silent and let the catastrophic scenario unfold before his eyes. Drops of sweat traced the fine lines on his temples. He was aware that he'd been completely wrong because the situation was now out of control. A frightened old man was sobbing like a child close to him, his pants soiled, and now here they were, surrounded by a hysterical crowd ready to attack. The fear of failure nailed the young officer to his seat. His self-esteem at half-mast, he didn't dare make eye contact with his colleague. These losers outside, ready to trash everything, disgusted him.

After a good fifteen minutes of nerve-racking status quo, the navy blue vans started to arrive in the housing project and the crowd dispersed for a while. But they gathered again in the middle of the principal artery, far from Moussa Traoré, Laurence da Silva, and their colleagues, who escorted Lucien Marchand to the police station.

In the neighborhood, the face-to-faces began, the imminent confrontation weighed heavily, attempts at mutual intimidation, the point of no return.

On one side, the riot police special force with all its crowd-control gear, all highly trained men, with their shields and coercive weapons firmly attached to their belts!

Sneakers against rangers. About one hundred yards away, a crowd of hooded adolescents, scarves beneath the eyes, rage in their gazes, ready to fight. One of them has made up his mind; it's Mouloud, drunk on testosterone. He moves up to about ten yards, jaw clenched, mouth open, a scream slips out:

—We can't take it anymore! Tonight, we're gonna burn everything, tonight, shit's gonna hit the fan!

~

Then a rainstorm of various types of projectiles comes crashing down onto the police shields of the officers lined up in tight rows. Burning objects, *pétanque* balls, bottles, stones.

~

Rosa Maria, an indifferent spectator to the fire in the neighborhood, strolls along, still consumed by the lukewarm love trickling down between her thighs. Project 6000 is once again in an uproar. The boys are all there, Mouloud, Jason, Mohammed, Pascal, Hamid ... everybody, no exceptions. She's known each and every one of them for years now. Like her, many of them were born in the neighborhood. Today, their faces are hard, their cheeks frozen, with venom on their lips and metal on their dilated pupils, their gazes are pumped up, radiating resentment!

~

She no longer sees them. Rosa Maria prefers to become invisible and fluid and to undulate toward the sky, to go far away, way beyond Paris and even the surrounding national highways, on a flying carpet launched at a steady speed, her mind slowly making a run for it, at which point she slows down, shivering at the memory of the embrace.

—What are you doing, Rosa? I told you to go home. Shit's gonna go down, the cops are coming down.

~

Deaf to his words, she smiles discreetly and keeps on moving slowly and calmly. Children are being harangued in the street, forces are gathering, rage is brewing, a danger, an avalanche, a cannonball.

~

In the middle of all the chaos, Rosa Maria takes off, ignoring the anger coming from her friends gathered in front of the entrance to the tons of concrete. She remembers the pleasure of Jason, his lower lip trembling, his eyes that closed after he came ... In Rosa Maria's belly, a rush of blood, a spark, is throbbing again, rising up toward her breasts, before spreading quickly throughout her entire body. Tingling sensations, a wave of pleasure, a heat wave that makes her shudder from the tips of her fingers to the roots of her hair and gives her the sweet sensation of balancing, without support, the soles of the feet posed gently on quicksand.

⬧

The steel lodged in clenched fists, cement in the legs. The projects has once again boxed itself in with its rings of expressways, somewhere far off the beltway. The complex is ecstatic, its sons are ready, an urge to fight and to shock pulsating in their whole beings! Police on one side, on the other, guys from the neighborhood originating from at least four continents, possessed by the same desire to exist, to exist … A new kaleidoscope, unique, hesitating, a crowd whose contours are unclear, galvanized, determined … Then an all-out meltdown.

⬧

The police, who up until this point had gotten down on one knee to brave the rage, suddenly rise up like one man! The order to attack is given. The police run, clubs in hand, visors lowered; they prefer to see just enough to distinguish, especially not to feel anything, no longer feel, reestablish the natural order of things, break bones, and destroy muscles. Impose silence and peace by beating on heads, systemically trampling on their demands, definitively silencing them beneath their boots. The return to normal is being prepared and will be systematic, precise, and final. Civil servants are on the job.

⬧

Rosa Maria is dreaming, she's on her way to someplace where there are beaches and sun. Intangible, she's leaving behind the despair, the violence, and the fire. Exiled in her dream, the girl is radiant.

⬧

Rage is circulating unabated and boiling in the veins of the projects, getting out of control and seeping into everything. A craving to massacre and destroy. The asphalt in the heart beats a haunting rhythm that comes together and makes a lump in the chest.

The streets won't be able to withstand the attack much longer; the meager forces of courage are falling apart before the organized and powerful surge of the police. And there is but one feeble trembling voice, choking far off, stifled hope:

—We can't take it anymore, we're going to break everything! Tonight it's ...

The showdown ends, handcuffs on wrists, with slaps in the face and insults, faces against the ground twisted into painful grimaces, knees planted into the backs of adolescents to prevent resistance. Club to the torso. Rage has failed, its face is projected against the wall in the back of the cells at the police station. Powerless before the unequal balance of power, the protest had been crushed, humiliated, momentarily reduced to silence.

Smoked, stripped, burned-out cars, spilled trash containers, businesses ransacked—the neighborhood of project 6000 will carry these marks like wounds for a long time. The scraps of an apocalyptic landscape, a sneak peek of the end of the world. In the middle, legitimate violence proudly parades.

～

Rosa Maria arrives in front of her building and bumps into Margarine, beside herself:

—Rosa, where you coming from? It's war out there, didn't you see?

Rosa Maria rubs her eyes and hesitates to return to reality.

—I saw ... it made me afraid.

—You're acting weird, Rosa. Did you smoke or what? I came out of the supermarket with your sister Sonia late afternoon when she'd finished work. She was the one who told me that the fascist pig in tower D, you know the old guy Lucien what's-his-name, the one who's always insulting Arabs and blacks, well, he went nuts and started shooting at everybody.

Rosa Maria remains unfazed.

—I swear! You know, apparently there were some young people on the sidewalk in front of Black Move, then there was some mix-up with the old geezer, who wanted them to scram. They insulted him, and he blew a fuse, he grabbed a piece and fired three or four times, I don't remember how many.

Rosa Maria would like Margarine to shut up, too many tragedies, blood and fire, she can't take it anymore.

—After, the entire neighborhood came downstairs. The guys broke everything, they burned cars and trash containers, some really crazy shit. That's why the cops filed charges, it got way out of hand. I think they arrested around fifteen guys! You should have seen it, those cops, all muscle, lined up against these tiny skinny kids in their sweat suits and sneakers . . . seriously crazy.

—Yeah, some seriously crazy shit . . . OK, Margarine, gotta go, I'm running late.

It's eight o'clock when Rosa Maria comes through the door. Her sister Sonia rushes up to her.

—Shit, Rosa, what the hell have you gone and done again? Have you seen what's going on outside? Mom is worried, and Dad's gone dead silent. I told him that you went to see a friend who's sick, to take her the homework. You hold it together now, we're going to eat.

Rosa Maria says good evening and sits down at the table in the dining room to the left of her father. Salvatore Milano, his wife, Angelina, and his three girls, Sonia, Rosa Maria, and Anna attentively watch the televised news that relates what just went down in a special report:

Integration, immigration. Lucien Marchand, retired military officer, maniac, a veteran of the colonial army was taken in for questioning, temporary insanity, remanded into custody, provocation, on the threshold of tolerance. French, of foreign origins. Law enforcement demonstrated exemplary courage, young people, looting, the riot police were deployed in great numbers throughout the notoriously difficult housing project and at the RER train station . . .

The special bulletin continues, integration, immigration . . . street scuffles at housing project 6000 . . . police . . . rioters.

Accompanied by images of veiled women crying, young dark-skinned or black people, eyes filled with hate, making threats in a disconcerting commotion, cars still burning in the parking lot. Riot.

The newscaster then abandons his dismayed expression, turns toward the left camera and addresses the spectators with a smile, white teeth perfectly aligned, ready for the weather report for the next day. Clouds, downpours in the north, and clear skies for the rest of the country!

~

Salvatore orders that the TV be turned off, dinner is ready.

—They should load them all up and send them back to the jungle, it's them and their rotten drug dealing that led my son to tragedy, degenerates, good-for-nothings, these young people, monkeys!

Rosa Maria, beautiful and strengthened by the love pulsating throughout her, tightens her fists around her knife and fork. She's drawing on a renewed courage that allows her to wear her head high, determined not to let injustice go on. Her expression gains confidence, she breathes deeply, turns her face to the right, and stares directly at her father. Rosa Maria is daring. Her legs shake a little bit, but she is stronger than ever:

—First of all, you're not more French than them, and plus they're not monkeys, they're my friends. Antonio liked them a lot too!

In the Milano household, time suddenly stops. Only little Anna keeps on eating as though nothing has happened. Angelina turns white and fears the worst:

—Be quiet, Rosa, you don't speak like that to your father!

Sonia adds:

—Shit, Rosa, shut it, goddamn it!

—But it's true, they're not monkeys, they're my friends. I l—

Salvatore gets up and slaps his daughter, his huge specialized worker's hand catching her white cheek. Rosa Maria falls to the ground. Anna screams and cries. Angelina blocks her ears, sobbing and shaking her head from left to right. Before her father's determination as he moves dangerously toward her sister crouched down, dazed, Sonia steps away. Rosa doesn't manage to dodge the kick to her side that lodges her back to the wall, suddenly blocking her breathing and doubling her over in two.

—Go on, get out of here! I don't wanna see you no more!

IN THE ROOM she shares with her two sisters in the back of the modest apartment, Anna opposite and Sonia in the lower bunk, Rosa Maria is still enjoying being half-asleep. Her cheek on fire and her ear still ringing, she is still shaken up from the events of the previous night and cradled in Jason's love, the first time, happiness finally. The fire in the housing project and some screams still haunt and frighten her. The blows from her father. She is hanging on relentlessly to the taste of his lips pressing on hers, the lights of Sicily, the Mediterranean Sea. Rosa Maria hears little Anna playing with her doll down below, she half opens her eye on the space that has become too cramped over the years. The aging furniture reduced to the bare minimum, a wardrobe of plywood in which the clothing for all three girls is piled, a chair and a table for schoolwork. The square room is ugly with a low ceiling. The sun, even though it is blindingly bright and high in the sky, barely penetrates the room. For each of the girls, intimacy is confined to the contours of her mattress. In the morning, the bedroom conceived for one person stinks of sweat and a strong musty smell.

Rosa Maria wraps herself up into her comforter and turns toward the wall in hopes of dreaming some more.

—Hey, wake up, Rosa, you can't be still sleeping? It's almost midday. Don't worry, you can come down and leave the room, the parents are gone, they won't be back before dinner.

Sonia busts into the room, she runs to the window and opens the shutters.

—Goddamn it, Rosa, because you're scared, you leave the little one playing in the dark! You should have seen it, it rained like crazy this morning. Luckily now it's almost beautiful out.

⮜

A draft of fresh air caresses the nape of Rosa Maria's neck while she lies on her belly. Her face, puffy from the night and swollen from all the blows, is still buried in the pillow she holds tightly between her bare arms. She gets up, squints her eyes a little bit from the sliver of sunlight, and wakes up slowly, slightly shivering, a bundle of nerves, surprised by the empty space beside her. In love, she is still moored to the most marvelous of dreams. Rosa would have loved that the next morning never came to pass, to remain under the illusion of living like a bird, light and carefree, sleeping and singing every day, flying above the complex, perched on a branch looking down on the world.

—Hey, Rosa, what came over you last night to make you talk to Dad like that? The next time, believe me, he's gonna kill you! You gotta really understand that between the unemployment, Antonio's death, and everything . . . it makes sense that he's on edge!

⮜

The images from yesterday are now coming into full view in her mind, the forbidden dance, the gunshots, Jason's magnificent body, the most beautiful she could ever imagine, the pain and then the pleasure in her belly, the ecstasy, the complex in flames, the attack by the police officers, everything. She'd like to lie down and escape in her sleep.

—We didn't do anything wrong, Sonia, I swear. Plus, after all, it's true, I can't let it be said that they're monkeys, they're my friends, they're really good to me.

—Your friends? They made a goddamn unbelievable mess. You gotta be really stupid to break everything in your own neighborhood, it was already ugly. Now, forget about it! You just have to look around. We don't even have a supermarket anymore, gotta go really far to do shopping, with bus tickets and everything, can you imagine the cost? My boss called me, I'm going to be transferred to Paris! Thank your friends, that'll mean more than an hour-long commute every day. I like your buddies, but honestly, we didn't need this!

—They're not the ones who fired the shots. It's only natural that they got angry, you gotta understand them too and not keep misjudging them.

—Well, OK, Rosa, we're not going to bicker about it. Come on, up you go, we've got housework and so on to do. Show me your cheek, holy shit the black and blue! The old man went right for it. You gotta really watch out next time. Go on, hurry up, I'll wait for you in the kitchen.

~

Rosa Maria climbs down from the bunk. She hears children playing outside, behind the building near the parking lots. They're all running around, bickering, she can't really tell if they're having fun or fighting. These kids are filled with so much life, pure energy, an explosion of enthusiasm in the middle of what's left of the mess. They're making comments about the events of Saturday with a strange kind of excitement.

—Did you see what happened yesterday, it was like war ... the older kids really fucked everything up ... It was awesome!

They're playing, their feet in the ashes that cover the whole street. They're dying to grow up and dream of one day imitating their idle elders, backs up against the walls of project 6000 or rear ends stuck to public benches, bored, spitting for hours on the ground, laughing, hanging together, and fighting with the police, push comes to shove.

Rosa Maria looks at them with tender eyes, she's dreaming of gold, of blue, of desire like an offering, a treasure, clear water, a caress that recalls the summer and the velvety feel of the volcanic dusty grounds beneath the soles of the feet.

LATER ON IN the afternoon, a group of boys gets together around the bench close to the football field. They assume the triumphant position of winners, shoulders upright and high, a serious attitude. They are the heroes of the day, the martyrs of Saturday night. Their faces are serious, the disorderly rants were silenced with clubs, but they dared, the projects had defied the authorities. The turmoil is still alive; it's beating a quick pulse under the pores of the skin, a biochemical disorganization that goes right to the brain, a storm in the making, uncertainty.

Further along to the right, toward what is left of the supermarket, a patrol of policemen with helmets is ready to intervene should it become necessary. The policemen walk in step, guns at their chests and the shields behind. They are maintaining a respectful distance to avoid any form of provocation. They advance within ten yards toward the bench to make their presence known then disappear to the right behind a building. The latest model sneakers grip the asphalt, the pressure of the thumb and the index finger become more apparent on the cigarette in the corner of the pinched lips. Necks stiffen. Muscles, sculpted during several hours in the makeshift fitness room in the basement, tighten suddenly. Nervous laughter. Rage is brewing again, outbursts of loud, uncontrolled voices:

—Goddamn it, they take us for clowns.

—Look at those bastards, they keep patting themselves on the back like last night ... They took advantage with their vans and all the gear, you would think they were in a movie. Is it a civil war or what here? Came with I don't know how many dogs, some of them even hit the kids, little kids, like Boubacar's brother. On my mother's life! Honestly, they hit him so many times on the head that he's in the hospital! Word, if they come close, those sons of bitches, I'm gonna let 'em have it, like yesterday, direct!

HAMID IS HEATED up, a bundle of nerves, ready to fight. He's looking for a way, an outlet for his anger, fists in his sweatshirt. He's also afraid, what if the police come back? Overexcited, he's shifting his weight from one leg to the other. Rage is still boiling, less intense than yesterday, maybe more dangerous because it's so contained, it's bad. The frustration of failure, the young people are on the losing side here. Jason adds:

—Goddamn it, first they go after Antonio, who wanted nothing to do with them. He was afraid of these motherfuckers, you know. After, that idiot smokes us like rabbits! Shit man, if the Good Man had been here, they would never have dared to close Black Move, he would have torched all their police cars. Holy shit, I wonder how they managed to get him!

—Personally, I think it was when he had his friends in Paris, he got too hot for them, he was getting too confident, oh yeah, on my mother's life!

Commotion sets in, the commentary starts melding into a confusing mess.

—Yeah, they should have let us kill that other motherfucking fascist pig, shit man, I would have so fucking killed him!

—They always protect the others, as if we were their dogs. We open a room to be able to party, all cool, and they come pulling guns on us. That's out of control, man, seriously.

—That's why Antonio was trying to dodge, he went to see the real guys in Paris, but even then, you see, they don't leave you alone!

—That's how it is, what do you think, on my mother's life, it's like that, there's nothing for us, no jobs, nothing, nothing but blows to the face, that's how it is, nothing you can do, it's all for them!

—Yeah, but we showed them yesterday, honestly, we really let 'em have it, bastards, sons of bitches, there were definitely some. We

Wilfried N'Sondé

seriously killed it, right, Mouloud? What did you do to the one who fell to the ground, you guys didn't catch it? Mouloud, he took him by the head, a blow with the knee, his helmet flew off. You would have thought it was a volley return, on my mother's life, he bled so much, nose, mouth, everything, after he finished him with some kicks with his shoes in the sides, balls, and everything, yeah, awesome, bro!

~

Taciturn until now, sitting with his legs open and his head hanging down to spit in peace, Mouloud raises his head when he hears his exploits being retold. The young man has a hard time hiding his smile and the little glimmer of satisfaction in his eyes. This is how he gets respect in the hood, when he's the strongest, the one who's giving and breaking... Not like in that nightmarish desert, not like over there where they did things to him that really hurt and that can never be forgotten.

He chases away the bad memories. Yesterday, it was he who won. One by one, palms go up in the air to him; he raises his own to meet theirs. Together, they laugh, congratulate each other, it's their victory, their celebration. Mouloud takes the floor:

—Hey, Jason, you two-bit stud, apparently you were the one who smashed the face of that nut bag with a bottle? Respect, brother!

—Stop, Mouloud, I seriously aimed, right for the teeth!

Jason is celebrating in the middle with the neighborhood guys and welcomes their friendly taps joyfully; he's just improved on his image again. The young people are laughing, mimicking some dance steps and combat sport moves. Everyone's doing what they're good at, they're exaggerating, getting the heart pumping...

—Bare hands, one against ten—we certainly showed them!

~

Suddenly, it's all calm, everybody goes quiet. An armored vehicle from the national police force advances, tinted windows, it goes by the supermarket then slows down, progresses slowly, and comes to a halt where the young people are standing.

~

—Slow down, Brigadier General, but be careful not to stop, otherwise stones could be thrown like yesterday. Good, like that, go slowly, just enough for the lieutenant to take a few shots.

Laurence da Silva is focused on the group gathered around the bench, every single one of them has turned toward her. Armed with her digital camera, she doesn't miss a single face.

—OK, Captain, that's great. I don't think I've forgotten anyone. We can go now!

—Speed up. Let's head back to the station. It's best not to be seen in the housing projects right now. Everything went well. Let's head back to the station and look over the pictures I took and see if we can identify the leaders.

∼

The young people follow the course of the armored vehicle, their eyes injected with blood.

—Bastards, sons of bitches, they've come to provoke us, and they don't even have the balls to get out of the car and have it out man to man!

BY THREE WEEKS later, calm has returned to project 6000. The nursery and the annex to the mayor's office resume their responsibilities. No incidents to complain about, and the riot police have stopped pacing up and down the neighborhood streets.

The police are waiting. The violence against law enforcement, the destruction of public buildings and of public property, and the assault of a police officer who fell to the ground will not go unpunished. The neighborhood must not be transformed into an area where the law cannot be enforced. A good number of the rioters have been identified. Captain Moussa Traoré, seconded by his colleague Lieutenant da Silva, is waiting for the right moment to take action. They are ready.

The fall season has already arrived in the neighborhood, and there is frost on the ground and on the buildings early in the morning, making them even sadder than usual beneath the low, dark skies. The cold has kept the young people off the benches; boredom has set in from long hours sitting in front of the TV in apartments that are too small for large families, or they're just hanging in the stairwell. The riot seems to have been forgotten. In any event, nothing has changed. Gloom, the daily routine of having no money, and idleness have all resumed their positions.

You can see Mouloud roaming around alone in the projects or sitting on the bench spitting and smoking cigarettes.

Behind the revamped bus shelter, there is no longer an ad, no more dreams of turquoise seas and half-naked Tahitian girls. It's the end of the day, it's already dark outside, and women and men returning from Paris descend from the bus in whatever which way they can.

~

Sonia notices Margarine. She hadn't recognized her before because her blond hair is hidden beneath a beautiful bright red beret, high heels, fishnet stockings, she's wearing a fantastic black coat that falls mid thigh length.

—Hey, Margarine, is that you? Holy shit, I can't believe it, you look so classy. What are you doing? We don't see you too much around here anymore.

—Hi, Sonia, I still come every once in a while to see my father and my buddies in the neighborhood . . .

She gives Sonia a wink and a knowing smile.

—But I work in Paris now, in a nightclub on the Champs-Élysées. The pay's really good!

—Oh yeah, you look so chic.

—Wait, you haven't seen my dress, come here, check it out.

They go about ten yards away from the crowd. Margarine opens her coat and shows off her gorgeous black dress, plunging neckline, refined velour, and a slit all the way up to the hips.

—Wow, it's so beautiful, fantastic . . . Wait, so what's your job?

Margarine bursts into uproarious laughter as she closes her coat:

—You know, my dear, I think you really don't want to know, but it's not going to last long, so let it go! By the way, what about Rosa, how's she doing? I heard that she's been sick.

—Yeah, Rosa, she must have caught a cold. What do you expect, it's freezing outside. She's been confined to bed for several days, but she refuses to go see a doctor . . . You know how Rosa can be, damn annoying.

—Hey, Sonia, you think I can go see her, a quick in and out?

Sonia hesitates:

—You know, I don't know with my father being so weird. I don't think he likes you too much!

—Mmm, not sure, you know . . . We can always try. It's no big deal if he throws me out, plus I won't stay too long.

—OK, let's go!

Three weeks of solitude, of suffering, and at times, of dreaming for Rosa Maria. Jason is avoiding her. They claim he is dancing mainly in Paris now, he's overbooked, and anyway, he doesn't want to see her. Her secret love, the memory of the delicious moment spent with him, she cherishes every second of her first time, the pain that was quickly replaced by escape, two bodies giving themselves to each other taking them into an unknown splendid universe, even more intense than what she had imagined. He is her man for all eternity. What she experienced is irreplaceable. For her, it's like they created a bubble for themselves, far from all the grime that surrounds them. He is here, everywhere, too bad if he doesn't want to have anything to do with her... He will end up changing his mind, and anyway, no one can take away her treasure, not even Jason.

Rosa Maria feels sick, exhausted, confined to her bed, her skin makes her suffer, a sudden heavy fatigue that persists, must be love pangs, she loves him so much. Hours go by, several days have gone by already, the nausea is torturing her, a whole uncontrollable and violent ruckus in her abdomen, the urge to constantly vomit, nothing comes out, a real ordeal. Maybe Jason will come by and visit her, he certainly doesn't know that she's sick. He'll come by, and she'll get well, together they'll take off hand in hand, protected by their union, to never leave each other again.

Her body is wounded, but hope is still alive. She's waiting.

Margarine and Sonia enter the apartment discreetly. They go by the open door of the kitchen. Angelina doesn't notice them, she's holding little Anna in her arms, sitting on the sofa watching a television game show.

In the back at the window, Salvatore slowly turns around. He glances and immediately recognizes Margarine despite her hat and her long black coat. Only a few seconds and it's always the same stirring. His legs are like cotton wool, images of flesh, sweaty palms, his heart is galloping away, heat in his head, a furnace in his body, uncontrollable desire. The crazy desire to relieve himself and dream, his head resting on her belly after the embrace, she awakens his thirst for sweetness and tenderness.

The young ladies rush into the bedroom in the back.

—Hey, Rosa, it's me. How you doing?

—Oh, Margarine, what a beautiful surprise.

Her voice is a bit hoarse, she has difficulty getting up and, in the light, reveals a much paler face than usual. Rosa Maria has gotten even skinnier, weak, her eyes have dark circles.

~

—Don't kiss me, I'm sick, I don't know what I have ... but, hey, look at you, you're looking pretty classy. Did you win the lotto or what?

—Yeah, a million! No, I have a new job for one more week, after that I'll be back, it pays well, that's all ... Oh my God, Rosa, you don't look too good at all, you need to see a doctor, this isn't good!

—Maybe Monday, if I'm still sick, we'll have to see. Have you seen Jason in Paris?

—No, I don't know where he hangs out there. Why? You still have it bad for him? Forget it, he's a player that's all, he sleeps with anything that moves! The guys around here are all lame, gotta forget him.

—No, he's a good guy ... So, Margarine, you still going down to the basement?...

Sonia interrupts her:

—Leave her alone, Rosa, it's none of your business! Well, come on, you gotta go, my parents are starting to go at each other's throats!

—OK, and don't worry, Rosa, I don't go down to the basement anymore, only to see my buddies and not for too long. Very soon, I'm going to get out of here. OK, ciao.

A dispute bursts out in the living room. Salvatore is upset and starts hurling insults at his wife, making big gestures and pointing an accusing index finger, threatening. Incredulous, surprised, she defends herself as best she can. She has no idea what he's talking about, until she catches a glimpse of her daughter Sonia opening the door to the one who looks to her like the neighborhood whore who used to go to Rosa's school.

SNUGGLED UNDER HER comforter in the depth of her bed, Rosa Maria is unable to fall back to sleep. The secret has robbed her of sleep for three nights already. Sometimes joyful, she stifles the giggles in her mouth; other times, seriously concerned, cold sweats, fear like a noose around her neck. Now she understands why she had the fainting spells that made her go twice to the school infirmary. The nausea that has been torturing her for ten days now is also clear. Her body is changing, her chest has become a little bigger, she's proud and feels like a woman for the first time. Rosa Maria is shaking, she's having a hard time finding the courage to tell Sonia, who is sleeping above her. She hasn't had her period, the test that she bought at the pharmacy was positive. Rosa Maria is expecting a baby, her and Jason's child. She hesitates, massages the corners of her lips with her thumb and index finger, and she dares to lean her head toward her sister, then in a low voice:

—Sonia, Sonia, wake up. I've got something to tell you, it's important, I'm scared, Sonia!

—Rosa, shit, you're annoying, let me sleep!

—It's really important, Sonia, you have to help me, I don't know how to get out of it. I'm afraid I'll do something really stupid!

Annoyed, Sonia suddenly gets up, rubbing her eyes, heads toward the table, and turns on the little bedside lamp before telling Rosa to come down and join her.

—What is it now, Rosa? Shit, now that you're not sick anymore, what is it? You're wearing me out!

Rosa Maria bends her legs and brings her knees under her childhood nightgown beneath her chin. She's gently rocking back and forth while passing her hands along her tibiae and whispering, her eyes lowered:

—I think I'm pregnant, Sonia ... I took a test three days ago.

—Oh shit! Pregnant? Are you sure? You don't even have a guy ... I thought you were a virgin, holy shit, Rosa, that's all we need!

Panicked, Sonia tries desperately not to raise her voice. She murmurs while carefully articulating each word, especially so as not to wake anyone, the walls of the apartment are very thin. Embarrassed, Rosa Maria has nothing more to add. She holds herself back from expressing her joy and the bursts of laughter when she imagines herself playing with a baby, chubby-cheeked with curly hair, chocolate colored, as sweet as can be, cute enough to eat and with a huge magnificent smile, the same as Jason when his thick lips separate slightly and light up his entire face. The embryo in her belly allows her to escape from the repeated dramas, the omnipresent violence, and especially the absence of Antonio, as well as the boredom. Thanks to the baby, she forgets and dreams again. Rosa Maria sees herself radiant, walking to the market on Saturday mornings among the other mothers, proud behind her stroller. Too bad that at their last meeting two days ago, Jason told her:

—What, what's all this mess about? You're pregnant, maybe I'm not even the father, go on, cut it out, that's enough! Figure out all this mess on your own, you should have paid attention, shit, birth control pills are not made for cows!

Then he went and joined another girl at the bus stop. Despite the contempt he shows her, she will always love him.

Sonia sits down, she takes her head in her hands and shakes it from left to right.

—Shit, Rosa, tell me this isn't true, you're all gonna make me go crazy in this family, it's just not true ... I can't believe it! It just can't be, honestly, it's not true, this isn't going to end well!

She gets up and looks closely at her sister with an insistent gaze:

—The father, Rosa? First of all, who's the father?

Rosa Maria lies down and places her hands on her heart, her throat knotted up in shame, feeling helpless, she recognizes the tense and nervous face her sister takes on when things go badly. The last time it was the death of their brother. There is no hope in Sonia's eyes, before which parade a squadron of catastrophic scenarios. Rosa doesn't recognize an ounce of approval, let alone compassion. She stutters:

—It was with Jason … you know, the one I like …

—What? That good-looking black guy, the one from the supermarket, the playboy who always hangs out in the building hallways and sleeps with all those sluts in the basement? My poor girl, you've got to be out of your mind. And a black guy, at that … No, but can you imagine us here with a black guy? Mom and Dad, the family in Sicily, can you see us showing up with some black guy? You've completely lost it, Rosa! They're great to have fun with, yeah, but, Rosa, not to have kids with, you've completely lost it, they're not like us, you know that yourself. Holy shit, you're completely nuts. That said, still glad it wasn't that other wacko, the Arab, Maboul or I don't know what you call him!

—Mouloud, his name is Mouloud, he's a friend, that's all, we talk, but Jason … I love him … plus, it wasn't in the basement … it was really amazing.

—Oh yeah, OK, you're not the only one he likes very much, that I can assure you … whatever! Shit, Rosa, this guy has nothing in his head, he thinks with his dick … Oh just shut it, Rosa!

On the brink of a nervous breakdown, Sonia suddenly sighs deeply; she has to think about it quickly and, well, first calm down. That kid, no way, there's no question of keeping it, shit! The older sister concentrates for a moment, no one must hear them. Her eyes are rolling every which way, fear mixed with anger. Disaster has hit its high point. Aside from the unemployment and all the other calamities that have come down on the family, they're going to have to live with the shame of having black people in their home?

—Rosa, you're completely crazy. Why do you think that I'm killing myself working as a cashier in some supermarket at the other end of the world? To feed black kids you're making with some loser? I left high school to help out the family, especially because of Anna and you, for God's sake, you completely screwed up … You don't realize, Dad's going to kill you, and as for Mom, the poor woman, with all the problems she already has, they're going to massacre you, cut you up into little pieces! You can't even begin to imagine, seriously, Rosa, this is the last thing we needed.

ROSA MARIA IS pale, nausea of another kind is now rising in her torso, this time it's coming from her chest and grinding everything from the inside, damaging the heart, a groan. Words are stuck in her throat, the young girl is sad, not a single sound manages to get out, not a single complaint. A grave and heavy silence comes between the two sisters during the night, a wall of silence. They can hear Anna breathing in her bed, an innocent breath, light. Rosa Maria has confided in her big sister. She closes her eyes, gently caresses her belly. Communing once again with her treasure. She imagines the tiny fingers of a newborn enveloping her index finger.

Exhausted, resigned, Sonia sighs and takes the hands of her younger sister in hers to tell her in a calm and relaxed voice:

—You know Rosa, there's nothing we can do, there's only one solution. You're going to have an abortion as soon as possible, I'm sorry!

—An abortion? Sonia, I can't do that, we don't have the right … and God … and the Virgin Mary, how can we do that? We can't do that, Sonia! Let me keep it, please, I'm sure he'll be sweet. I'll look for a job too, so much for Sicily, I'll go somewhere else, please Sonia, let me keep it!

~

Tears pour down from Rosa Maria's eyelids, a river, a torrent, a deluge of distress; her face comes undone, expresses horrific pain. Rosa Maria, abandoned again. She wasn't expecting jumps for joy but was at least hoping for some understanding, a little bit of compassion and the chance to share her happiness with someone. Sonia, irritated, frightened as well, puts a hand to her mouth:

—Shit, Rosa, stop complaining, they're gonna hear you, control yourself for God's sake! It's going to be OK, don't worry, we'll sort it out with the help of the good Lord. When it's serious, he understands. And this is serious. I swear, you can't keep it. We'll make the appointment together, you're a minor, I don't think we'll have to pay anything, you won't even need to give your name. The Madonna forgives too, I'm sure of it. I'll go and pray with you, promise ... don't cry like that, shit, let's go, come on!

◆

Sonia, protective, takes Rosa Maria in her arms and brings her head against her chest. As quietly as possible, they sob together in the night, both of them lost, voiceless. Some time goes by before Sonia turns out the light. Rosa Maria climbs into the top bunk. Neither of them sleeps, silent in their pain, lulled by the distant echo of car engines on the state highway ... The death knell has sounded on Rosa Maria's world.

After several weeks of investigations led by Captain Moussa Traoré and Lieutenant Laurence da Silva, the police can finally take action.

About fifteen residents from project 6000, between sixteen and twenty-one years old, have been arrested in the mist and cold of the early hours of a November morning, without incident, without conflict.

⁓

The echo of the events of the raid, like a whirlwind on Sunday morning, is all everybody's been talking about for days, in the schools, in the market, at the counter of the betting shop. The regulars at the bar, like Salvatore, rejoice, these little assholes deserved a good lesson, in any event, that would teach them not to go around breaking everything and wreaking havoc. They need to be punished and made to understand the real value of things instead of spending their time loitering. As times passes and glasses keep getting refilled, opinions and proposals keep on coming:

—To the army, personally, I'd send all these kids to the army, that'd make men of them, real ones, not these little pricks who just do nothing but piss everyone off, these shitty little good-for-nothings!

In the line at the child welfare office, in the fruit and vegetable aisle, or at the fishmonger's section in the supermarket, some mothers are worried about the fate of their incarcerated sons. They have a hard time pulling themselves together after the police came barging into their apartments with their heavy-handed search warrants, searching the bedrooms, despite their screams, crying, and pleas.

Incredulous, they will struggle for a long time with the unbearable memories of the terrorized expressions on their sons' faces as they were being taken away, handcuffed behind their backs, heads down, in the middle of all these civil servants who forcibly took them in. Hours in police custody, without any reassuring information. During the wait, these mothers vacillate between the worst and the hope that their little ones will return home soon. Anxiety disrupts their sleeping habits and eats away at their hearts.

New excitement animates the paths of project 6000. Young people brave the November cold to talk, they're chatting on the benches, some are whispering in the basement.

It took ten minutes for the plainclothes officers to apprehend the suspects. Some got into the vans, shoes unlaced, pajamas showing under their jackets. They took in the youngest ones.

In the entrance to Rosa Maria's building, the heroes of the riot are alarmed and start speculating. Doubt and fear take over, the oppressive feeling that a noose is tightening up. The words are grave:

—Holy shit, it's only the guys who were with us that they've arrested! The dealer assholes, who sell their poison to the kids, they leave them be, they're only giving us a hard time! And if the young ones give us up? Serious, they're all going to come down and take us in one by one, on my mother's life!

—Yeah, they've really fucked us, they came, they slapped us around and then just took off … and now one by one they're coming to get us … I swear they're doing it when we're all alone … It's crazy, but personally, fuck this shit, I'm outta here.

Sitting at the top of the stairs, Mouloud has spent a long time listening to the others, hands still on his knees, legs apart to watch the trickles of his spit, dry clicking his tongue and lips, maybe a little bit more nervous than usual given the tension in the air. He imposes silence by taking the floor:

—Assholes, shut up. Personally, I'm sure they're doing this deliberately to get us all riled up … and that's how they're going to catch us, of course! Come on, think about it for a minute! They're clever, what are they looking for exactly? ... I really can't figure it out.

Everybody goes quiet, intrigued by the difficulty Mouloud has expressing his ideas, hard to know if he's speaking to someone or if he's just thinking out loud.

At the same time, Sonia opens the door for Rosa Maria. With her hand on Rosa's back, Sonia follows her movement till she's inside.

—Hey, guys, can't you go hang out somewhere else? You just keep dirtying everything around here with your spit, your cigarette butts, unbelievable, such pigs!

～

Sonia's patience has reached its limit, irritated by the wait at the family planning center with her sister to schedule the abortion, she's about to implode. She can no longer bear the sight of these lazy boys.

—Hey, bitch, watch how you talk to us, who do you think you are? Does the building belong to you now or what?

Sonia becomes tense, ready to jump down someone's throat. Mouloud steps in and gives a slap to the back of the neck of the teenager.

—Hey asshole, watch your mouth, yeah, show some respect! We're gonna take off, girls, don't worry. You OK, Rosa? You don't look too good.

—I am sick, Mouloud, but it's going to be OK, thanks.

—No problem, Rosa, I'm here when you're ready. If you need anything, come and see me, OK, later! I'll be at the bench in a little while.

Mouloud leaves the entrance with the others. Sonia and Rosa Maria climb the steps of the staircase to the second floor.

—What do you and Antonio see in this guy? He's completely fucked up, have you seen his eyes? It's because of people like him that he wound up doing stupid things, Antonio. That guy, Mouloud, he followed Antonio everywhere, be careful, Rosa, I am serious!

—You don't know him, Sonia, that's all. He doesn't talk a lot, he listens, he doesn't judge people, you know, he's kind.

～

Later on, Rosa Maria meets up with Mouloud sitting on the bench in the early evening darkness. Alone, with his head down, he's smoking.

—You cool, Rosa?

—I dunno. I'm not doing so great, and you?

—It's OK, it's just the cops, they've started up again with their pestering.

He spits a little bit more discreetly than usual so as to not annoy his friend, then he dares:

—Who got you pregnant, Rosa?

Suddenly panicked, Rosa Maria raises her head up abruptly, her face veers to bright red in a matter of seconds, her neck has already betrayed her with red blotches of nervousness. Her eyes are rolling at full speed, disaster. She bursts into tears. A long sobbing in her soul, a real ordeal, the failed hope in her belly calls to mind a shipwreck. Of her lover, all that remains is a quiet moan from morning till night. Her chocolate baby, a creation of desire, of flesh and blood, is condemned. The little baby she imagined in her arms on a sandy black beach far away beneath the sun will never see Sicily.

⁓

Rosa Maria is consumed by fear, longing to die, completely confused with her feelings, paralyzed by the impossibility of being able to tell her parents that she gave herself to a black guy who never wanted anything to do with her or their child. It was crazy to imagine that she could have raised it alone, or with Margarine, her best friend, the only one who takes the time to listen to her and offer her tenderness and affection.

Sometimes when she allows herself to dream again, Rosa Maria loves the feeling of being pregnant, it gives her the courage to face the whole world. When her period was late, at first, she was frightened, but then she prayed to the Virgin Mary. The test confirmed in no uncertain terms that a life was blossoming inside her belly, the fruit of her union with Jason. At the time, she'd experienced a strange feeling, a mixture of joy for having achieved such an important moment, of rare beauty, and fear of the unknown.

Her satisfaction rapidly faded. She already suffers under the weight of the responsibility, alone, with no help before an insurmountable mountain, consumed on a daily basis with sophisticated schemes to hide her condition from the world.

The young girl has lost sleep from thinking so much and with no way out, a complete shambles in her womb and the nausea that keeps bringing her back to reality. More at ease being discreet, Rosa Maria is afraid of drawing attention to either herself or the baby, getting stares and becoming the target of ridicule and mockery. Even Margarine will reproach her and dissuade her from keeping the child.

—I can't take it anymore, Mouloud, I'm at the end of my rope, I feel like dying!

—Calm down, Rosa, don't cry like that! Personally, my mother told me … you know she comes from a small village … it's in the whites of the eyes that she sees these things … You understand? If there's a kid in a woman's belly or not … When she can take a good look at the shape of the belly, she can even tell you if it's a girl or a boy … Word! At your house, she saw it immediately, that's why I'm asking you … but I'm the only one … Don't worry … those other assholes don't see anything!

Mouloud pauses to find the right words, feeling emotional and a little bit overwhelmed by the situation, he ventures a remark:

—You're a nice girl, Rosa … You should have waited to get married before doing it, don't you think?

Between two hiccups, Rosa Maria tries to justify herself, with little success. She's losing control, saddens, scratches her face, her wrists pound on her legs and her chest. Staring off into space, she answers:

—You know, Mouloud, I loved him for quite some time, with him it was beautiful, like magic … and now I don't know anymore, everything is weird in my head … I'm afraid, Mouloud, I'm afraid!

—Why didn't you say anything to me, Rosa? I mean, we know each other, I'm like your brother now. Since when have you been going with this guy, who is he? Is it one of those guys from project 6000?

Mouloud turns toward Rosa and gives her a serious look, almost paternal. She blushes, tears inundate her face, but he still finds her beautiful with her thick black curly hair. Mouloud finds that even with features marked by distress, her face has a unique charm. Sadness gives her a grave and profound air, her eyes sparkle against her pale complexion. With hesitant fingers, he fixes a rebellious strand of hair caught between her lips.

Mouloud's question puts an end to the illusions. Rosa Maria returns to being the little shy and shameful girl. Jason had never loved her! He's no longer the young man she embraced passionately in her dreams above the cliffs in Sicily, between the azure of the skies and the immense blue of the Mediterranean. The one she held, hand in hand as they ran along on the black sandy beach, their feet in the saltwater, before stopping, feeling happy, protected, immersed in love in the shelter of his arms.

—Sonia's right, I have to have an abortion … It's better!

Horrified, Mouloud gets up and grips her by the shoulders:

—No, no, Rosa, even with your God, you don't have the right … You'll immediately go to hell, don't do that! What does your boyfriend think?

Rosa Maria hesitates to answer. She gathers up her courage, her voice is cold and disturbing.

—Jason is not my boyfriend … We only slept together once at his aunt's place in block E, the day things heated up in the neighborhood … I'm not going out with … The baby, he couldn't care less … he doesn't want to have anything to do with me, he never wanted to have anything to do with me!

The words of her pain plunge her into long seconds of absence and silence, interrupted by Mouloud's tongue smacking between his lips. Rosa Maria's mouth is dry. Her throat too. She sighs, not daring to look at him.

His friend's final sentence is causing Mouloud to get angry.

—Goddamn it, he didn't respect you! Asshole, son of a bitch, if I get a hold of him, he's not going to be looking good for a while, I swear, I'm gonna fuck him up … Shit, I'll get him, I swear I will …

Terrified before the fist he's making tighter and tighter, panicked by the violent impulse transforming Mouloud's face, Rosa Maria is frightened, starts sobbing again even more intensely, and begs:

—No, Mouloud, promise me, please, swear to me that you won't hurt him, promise! It's not his fault, it was me who wanted it, for a long time. I'm alone. In three days, I'm going to have an abortion, I'm afraid, I don't know what to do anymore, you gotta help me!

He calms down and swears on the Koran and on his mother's life that he won't ever touch Jason. He'll do it for her because she's a nice girl. He's going to help her get through this, like a big brother.

The young man's words calm Rosa down. Relieved, she rests her thick head of hair on Mouloud's thigh.

Having had a harsh upbringing, with no tenderness whatsoever, he stiffens a little bit, surprised, not knowing what to do with his hands, suspended in the air. He spits and then places two fingers on the warm nape of Rosa's neck. She responds with a sigh of relief, her muscles relax from his caress. Mouloud has the impression that Rosa's skin and black curls come to meet his palm. The atmosphere is pleasant despite the cold, she lays her arms on his legs, lets herself go for a few seconds. Rosa Maria forgets the weight on her shoulders. Mouloud consoles her with affectionate, simple, and new touches. He now has a gentle reassuring voice for Rosa:

—It's OK, Rosa, you'll see, it's going to be OK, I'm going to take care of it. You're going to go home, no fighting with the old man, I'm going to take some time and think about what we're going to do, we'll get through this, Rosa!

—Thank you, Mouloud, thank you!

After four kisses and a tight hug, Rosa Maria heads back home. Mouloud sits alone on the bench close to the football field.

Once again, his ability to understand is disrupted by distraction and the gravity of the situation. It's like he's chasing his own thoughts. This is a delicate matter, it concerns two lives, he's got to concentrate.

In his silence, he's wearing a disturbing expression. Mouloud is having a hard time gathering his thoughts. He's got to avoid getting angry, that extremely violent tendency he came back with from serving in the military.

He thinks about his mother, the person he cherishes the most in the world, a distant love with no physical contact since his childhood. She taught him to submit completely to paternal authority and bend over backward to give in to the tiniest of his demands. Her firstborn, and a boy at that, he reigns like a prince in the maternal world, even if every now and then she reprimands him severely when he dares to ask for a little affection. This is the price he has to pay now to one day become, himself, a stern, severe, and respected patriarch.

His time in primary school had ended pretty quickly with a resounding failure. His parents expected him to reign terror over his sisters and keep an eye so that they were exemplary in their social conduct because the whole family's honor depended on their virginity for marriage. His school life came down to an overview of learning to read and write. The teaching staff and the head of the school had together decided that his disastrous grades were the result of a neurologically related disorder that exceeded their resources. Furthermore, his behavior was a permanent menace, not only to other students, but also to the teachers. So he was sent home.

By the time he was legally an adult, he had already accumulated ten years of laziness and didn't understand much about the world or other people, but he had succeeded at becoming a real nightmare for his sisters and was his mother's pride and joy.

The army though had broken his soul. He struggled daily with the painful memories, a very deep trauma. Episodes from this sad period haunt him even on those days he spends hours sitting alone on the bench. At night, images of defilement poison his sleep. He's permanently spitting, probably to evacuate repressed impurities. While he has no real friends since Antonio's death, he's still pretty well known in project 6000. He and the deceased had formed a rather unusual duo, one always joyous and dynamic, the other awkward, reticent, and quiet. Mouloud had let himself be taken along the path that Rosa Maria's big brother had carved out.

⁓

Mouloud is thinking about Rosa, whom he's known forever. He has strong feelings for her, secrets he can't really explain, just a real desire to be close to her, as much as possible, he wants things to go well for her and nothing bad to happen to her. He appreciates her presence, the girl is so different, always kind, never vulgar. Rosa is the only one who will take fifteen or thirty minutes to keep him company. Sometimes, they don't even say anything to each other, just sit for a little while next to each other. She dreams, he smokes and spits. And then, Rosa is his buddy's baby sister, he feels responsible and mutters:

—It's about respect!

How can you help a girl who's pregnant? Mouloud is focusing. He can't sleep through the night. He sweats even though it's cold, his pulse is beating like crazy. Find a solution. She deserves a life like … He's looking for the word … Mind-blowing yeah, like when you're feeling good and your head turns a little bit, just enough, as if there were bubbles inside, like a sickness but that does a lot of good.

He'd had a day like that on the bank of the Seine with friends not so long ago … It was a picnic, no one spoke, the guys just watched the water gleaming. Rosa, he's got to offer her a life where she doesn't even feel the ground when she walks, he's gotta take care of her like she deserves, yeah. There's got to be water, sun, for the baby, that's what's best, and no towers and not too many highways. The child shouldn't grow up to become one of those asshole dealers, no, no, never! He should be laughing. Mouloud understands that the best thing to do is to leave, get away from the neighborhood, maybe move just a little farther out, over there where there are no more projects, beyond Paris. He looks at the bridge on the freeway, the steel, the concrete, much closer, the state highway, all around rectangular bars, the supermarket just in front of his eyes and, to the right, the bus stop. The ad might not be there anymore, but the image is carved into his head!

The sun, the pretty woman, her generous hips and smile, the beach, and the calm turquoise sea. The clear blue sky, palm trees, the good life, someplace else, over there where the days go by gently, barefoot in the sand, heat wave, the island at the end of the world, Bora-Bora, to start all over from scratch! Clearly, that's where he should take Rosa and her baby.

MOUSSA TRAORÉ AND Laurence da Silva now know the identity of the young people who took part in the riots, the fires, those who threw dangerous objects, and especially the person responsible for the bottle of beer that was thrown at Lucien Marchand. Several witnesses have confirmed that it was a certain Jason Lafleur, eighteen years old, employed, French, born in the department of Guadeloupe, with no criminal record. The individual who went after the riot police officer who fell to the ground has also been identified. Mouloud Zayed, twenty-five years old, no known profession, French, born in Paris.

MOULOUD WALKED AND reflected all night long. He's convinced of it: Bora-Bora will be the beginning of a new life. First, he walked all over the neighborhood, for several hours, then, at dawn, he paced the dirt roads between the fields on the other side of the state highway. Morning came, the young man put his thoughts together, he knows more or less what he's going to say to Rosa, now he's only got to find the right words to talk to her. Mouloud retraces his steps. A fleet of police vehicles go by on the main road. He's not paying attention, his mind is elsewhere. Mouloud gets back to the complex at about ten o'clock. In the state Rosa's in, she's got to be home … He sends a friend of her little sister to ask Rosa to come down and meet him on the bench. Minutes go by, he's smoking his last cigarette.

—Hey, Mouloud, what's up?

—You OK, Rosa, everything cool? You weren't sleeping, at least?

—No, you know there's all this nonsense going on in my head, it's going to explode, for sure! Plus the nausea and all that mess, I'm not sleeping, but I'm really tired!

After kissing him hello, Rosa Maria sits down beside him, her shoulders shudder and she huddles up, it's cold and humid. Mouloud is energized by the new prospects, overcome with joy, carried away by the thrill of taking off to the island of happiness.

—I know what we're going to do to get through this, Rosa, we're going to go really far away from here. You love the sea, right?

—It's funny that you should ask that, of course I love it. When I was a kid, we would go to Sicily, that's my island, the sea is so beautiful over there, blue and everything, and we always had our feet in the sand ... But with my pregnancy, it's not worth it, they'll kill me over there, they're worse than my father.

—Me too, I know about an island, I swear. There was that ad at the bus stop, do you remember it?

— ... No, I don't recall.

—One day, I even saw a TV report on it, that's where we have to go, word, for the baby and you and all, yeah, you'll be OK over there, you'll get your color back.

—Mouloud, is it far? How is it over there?

—Well yeah, it's far because it's like a thing you can escape to, you know. It's an island that's really stunning on the other side of the world, it's like you're walking upside down, it's called Bora-Bora. It's so great, with really fine, completely white sand, blue sea, really special, you can see the fish through it, you have every single color, yellow, orange, green, I swear, Rosa, I saw them on TV, on my mother's life! Can you imagine the two of us with the little one? That's where we have to go, Rosa, it's going to be so good, oh yeah! Apparently when the explorers discovered the island, they thought they were in paradise, well, I don't believe that, it's not good to say that, but it means that it's really classy, that's all!

Rosa Maria already feels the pleasant tingling of the sun burning her skin, her chocolate baby dressed in white, together they are floating in an immense, calm, crystal clear ocean, lying comfortably on a bed of algae and moss, alone on a huge beach in the Pacific Ocean, surrounded by wild flora. She listens to Mouloud and takes off with him. Rosa Maria closes her eyes, the ugly gray towers in project 6000 have disappeared, the horizon opens up, she forgets the state highways, the bridges, the cars, and the trucks. A mild wind takes her on imaginary paths filled with exotic flowers in her nose, the music of sparrows high up in the sky, the sounds of the tide smashing against the cliffs, a certainty of being elsewhere and living well, the desire to travel, a one-way ticket with no possible return to the filth, the dream of a new destiny with her child and Mouloud, a big brother, someplace else, on the other side of the world, to be on the opposite side of what she has always known. Simple days of freedom, peace, and love.

Rosa Maria snuggles up against his shoulder:

—Yes, Mouloud, please, take me right away wherever you want, so long as it's good and warm ... You'll take me, right, Mouloud, for real?

—Great, Rosa, you're a really nice girl. You know, your brother, Antonio, had told me a secret, he also wanted to get out of here, that's why he'd got into doing some business, and he even had a girlfriend, he was in love but he never said who it was!

—Poor guy, he never had a chance to leave ... Take me far away, Mouloud!

—Go on home, Rosa. I'll take care of everything!

With a little leap, Rosa Maria gets down from the bench, gives Mouloud a long hug, and heads home. He finds himself all alone, feeling emotional. So much tenderness and enthusiasm, something very difficult for his disturbed mind to digest. He loves this unique situation with Rosa, these unfamiliar feelings make him feel good. On the other hand, he's taking her pregnancy very seriously, which means that he has to act fast, for the well-being of both mother and child. He tightens his fists to give himself the courage, he swears to make it all happen and to protect them!

MOULOUD TRIES TO make a list of what both he and Rosa will need to go away. First problem, huge, money, a snag in his plans, a serious obstacle. He hunches his head into his shoulders, pushes his fists into the jacket to his sweat suit, and starts to pace up and down. Leaving for Bora-Bora or anywhere else requires money, but he has none. He's the man, the oldest, his first role is to be able to provide for his family. He's focusing, how's he going to get some? His last paycheck, a paltry sum for a soldier in the desert. No, he dismisses the memory of it, he needs to give this his full attention, an inspiration. Unemployed for a long time, his father doesn't work anymore either. He won't do a woman's job like his mother, who does housecleaning, or his sister Fatima, who washes the asses of sick people in the hospital. Mouloud squints his eyes and frowns. Ideas are coming together and bouncing around in his muddled brain.

Suddenly, the sound of hurried steps shakes him out of his slumber; it's Boubacar, the hairdresser.

—Shit, man, Mouloud, I've been looking everywhere for you, the police too, what the hell you doing here? They went by your place, searching it and everything, fuck man, you're a real top dog, boss man now! As for Jason, they took him in with the other guys this morning pretty early! That asshole, apparently he was crying like a girl, a real jerk!

Mouloud is dazed, his knees buckle, he stumbles a moment before leaning on the bench to regain his balance, and then sits down.

Shortness of breath, a huge weight on his chest, speechless, the blood leaves his face, pale, he stares into space, at the breaking point.

—What, you don't know? Where were you? Be careful, they're patrolling in every corner. There's so much hate, I swear. In my opinion, someone from the neighborhood ratted because I don't see how they could've got Jason, someone had to have told them about the bottle. Son of a bitch, if we catch whoever ran their mouth, we're gonna skin them! Watch yourself, bro, oh yeah! You gonna go into hiding or what?

Mouloud is no longer listening. His eyes are open, but he doesn't recognize anything. He needs silence, some quiet, some time to really take in this information. The activity in his head has momentarily stopped, suspended. First, he needs to clear his head. Stop the crazy blood racing, beating on his temples. He gets up without answering, ignores Boubacar, whom he looks at like a complete stranger, then covers his head with his hood before taking off.

Later on, in the early evening, after dinner, Salvatore decides to take a walk. He leaves his building and strolls toward the periphery of the projects. It's still early but already dark, pretty ideal to not be seen. Rosa Maria's father moves slowly on the rare low-cut grass area between the parking lot and the safety rails of the freeway. His gaze follows the sinuous contours of the asphalt decorated with full or dotted white lines, further along the roundabout and the bridges.

Salvatore rekindles his memories to avoid thinking about the young woman. He hopes she's come back and is waiting for men down in the basement. He imagines the tender hours next to her, a bit of company and sweetness. Skin firm and tight, generous curves, shapely, ready to satisfy his desire. Madness consumes him ...

He observes project 6000, standard concrete architecture near Paris, a landscape of questionable taste in the middle of the plain, at the center of an intersection of state freeways and surrounded by grain fields. Everyone lives next to each other, one on top of the other, no privacy, very little hope of hiding.

A lack of privacy, that's the real culprit, throwing this barely clad girl right in front of him and cramming his head with twisted ideas, a kind of sickness, a spell of pouting lips, skirts too short in the summer, making it all too easy to imagine the lace and the torrid smells where the skin is moist and delicate.

～

It wasn't so long ago that the kid was still having fun with Rosa in the kids' playground, close to the annex to the mayor's office, on the swing, the steel slide, or running around the concrete Ping-Pong table.

Get away from her, forget that image, stay loyal to Angelina, devoted wife of so many years. Take the opposite direction away from the basement. But Salvatore continues toward the Pablo Neruda school complex, a complex with a kindergarten and a playground separated from those belonging to the primary and middle schools. On the other side of the street, the father looks at the secondary school, a flat building, a block in the shape of a parallelogram, of discouraging austerity. The multipurpose room juxtaposed to the main building, constructed with provisional materials, has stayed like that for thirty years.

He struggles against the desire to plunge his face, at least one time, into the blond hair and close his eyes while taking in its perfume. Relive a moment of sensual pleasure. Lose his mind to the sound of the groans in cadence with the pleasure ... Whisper loving words as he becomes intoxicated by the savor of sweat.

Salvatore recalls the mornings, coming home, after dropping the kids off at school, they were pretty young then. He would take the day off to accompany everybody. Angelina prepared the youngest of them, shampoo and Savon de Marseille on every body part, even the inaccessible ones. The little girls held back the tears when the time came to use the unforgiving comb through the length of the mops of curly black hair. Their clothes, in tip-top shape, just like for Sunday mass, were obligatory, new, navy blue, white. That period when things were going well before unemployment, adolescence, drugs, the death of his eldest ... Then everything went to hell. The gestures of love are sorely missing, the longing, his inner muscles are stiff, his bones frozen.

~

The obsession rises up again and blurs the memory of the fifty-something-year-old man. The attraction persists, irresistible. Salvatore is hoping to be resuscitated by the contact with Margarine's pulpous lips. He swallows saliva, taking in the idea of the beautiful naked body beneath the blond hair, fragile and ready. In his desire, he imagines the embrace, a languorous body-to-body contact, him rubbing his poorly shaved cheeks, his paunch, his small waist, and the wide neck on his narrow shoulders on the girl's soft skin.

Salvatore inhales on the end of his cigarette butt for a long while, his throat, his lungs, the world around him drowns in a cloud of nicotine-flavored smoke. He coughs noisily and spits on the asphalt. His decision's been made, he advances, heavy-footed, inelegant toward the basement of tower F!

MOULOUD HAS BEEN hiding out for several hours in the darkest corners of the complex ... thoughts more confused than ever. Rosa. He promised her he would take her away from here, the baby, the riot police waiting for him at his parents' home, those bastards, Bora-Bora, the shame for his family, the white sandy beaches, his mother's tears, the magical reflection of the sun on the Pacific Ocean, the dishonor for his father, the blue sky at the end of the world ... The police on his heels. The urge to scream. Money. He hides behind the angle of a building and raises his eyes, his gaze lingers on the crescent moon. Steps come closer to him, faster, haltingly, heels clicking sharply on the asphalt. His pulse is racing again, Mouloud presses his back against the wall, weakened kneecaps, a violent discharge of adrenalin rises up in his torso, he closes his eyelids, someone's there. He has to save Rosa, it's his duty, she needs him. Terrified, the young man bites his lip until it begins to bleed, a pearl-shaped tear at the corner of his eye. Courage, don't flinch. She's very close to him, maybe five yards or more, he dares to look while staying hidden.

Margarine, blond hair flowing loose, black coat and fishnet stockings, descends the steps of the little staircase that leads to the basement. She quickly opens the door decorated with graffiti and disappears inside.

A few moments to regain his breath, Mouloud calms down. He's thinking, this time really fast. He just got a glimpse of Rosa Maria's friend, she'll be willing to help him. Farther along, a group of young people he doesn't know settle onto a bench. From that distance, they can't make him out. Fear of being busted. Unsure of his footing, he heads for the exit Margarine used. In turn, Mouloud descends into the basement. He closes the door behind him without making a sound, follows a faint light, and walks along practically feeling his way amid foul-smelling odors. Having played hide-and-seek here many times, he knows this place pretty well. The smell of a burning cigarette leads him directly to his target.

Once he plants himself in front of the frame to the door, Margarine absentmindedly turns her head and gives him a cold stare with eyes from which tears have just been dried, of dreams and illusions.

—What d'you want?

Margarine fixes the cloud of blue smoke she's just spewed out beneath the shade of her little bedside lamp. She automatically follows the slow round movements that dissipate into the air and filter the dust. The smoke reminds her of the logs that burn in a fire-place, like in a chalet somewhere in the Savoy mountains, childhood vacations.

She is sitting on a wooden stool near the mattress on the ground, absent, exhausted, lost. Her hairdo is in place. Margarine leans her elbows on her bare thighs under a bright red miniskirt, high up on her hips. Her black lace tank top barely hides her big chest, she is not wearing a bra. Her voice snaps sharp and final:

—What is it you want now? Go away!

—Oh, it's OK, I got something to ask you.

—What? You too, I can't believe this . . .

The disgust and contempt written on her pupils, Margarine gets up and lets out a huge cynical laugh. In this moment, she hates Mouloud and the whole world. She takes her breasts in her hands with a deliberate obscene pout, her tongue on her lower lip:

—You want to fuck, eh, is that it? Then come, at least you can pay?

She comes closer to him, provocative, places a hand on his zipper.

—So Mouloud Zayed, I'm no longer a slut for you, a whore that should be stoned? You check me out all the time as if I were something filthy, you say shit about me to Rosa, and when it's time to get off, you play all sweet and nice.

—Cut it out, shit! Damn, we know each other, word, I didn't come for that, I swear on my mother's—

—No, Mouloud, you don't know me anymore ever since I'm a whore, you're not worth much more than the others, your shit principles with your sisters, your women, and your mothers, then you want to come here to get blown, go on, get out, Mouloud, you disgust me!

～

Mouloud already regrets having come by, nothing is going as he had hoped, countless thoughts are confusing him. He blinks his eyes faster and faster to try to gather his thoughts. He panics. His right hand begins to tremble. He finds himself in a basement with a half-naked whore who's yelling at him like his father and the officers over there, back in the desert did, long before her. His brain is jamming up. The images of the soldiers in uniforms, the color of the sand, suddenly appear in his thoughts; it's all happening too quickly. He feels the burn from the paternal slap on his cheek mixed in with the daily bullying in the barracks, the flashbacks scramble around at full speed before his eyes, kicks in his sides from the officer, orders barked in a language he doesn't understand well, he's on the ground screaming, the humiliating fondling in the shower, Mouloud is losing it. With his sleeve, he wipes the sweat from his forehead, trying to stay lucid. Something is stinging his eyes. He manages to focus by thinking of Rosa, the baby, the sun on the beach, Bora-Bora, indulge yourself, get away!

Margarine is standing right in front of him, her breath on his face, she sputters the words on his mouth:

—Come on, Mouloud, come fuck, if you got the money. Come on!

—I'm not here for that shit, on my mother's life, you gotta help me … I need some money!

Margarine steps back in disbelief. She watches him, speechless, mouth wide open:

—What d'you want? I gotta be dreaming, you want me … me, to give money to you, the dough I make with my ass?

—I just want you to help me, you know, it's all ...

Mouloud lowers his head. He's sincere, his voice is low and plaintive.

—You poor thing, you really are a sick guy, you really need to get some help! You're a piece of shit, nut job, you're not even worth my whore money, go on now, get out!

—I need the money to get far away from here ... with Rosa and the baby she has in her belly. We're going to go to Bora-Bora ... It's really far ... There's the beach, the sun, and everything, over there we're going to be OK, the three of us ...

His enthusiasm gives Mouloud a bit of light and rekindles hope in his expression; he gathered the courage to reveal himself. He's feeling hopeful.

— ... Where do you want to go with Rosa? She's expecting a baby? Did you rape her or what? She has no business being with a head case like you, I'd already told her, what did you do to her? Already you were the one who dragged her brother into your bullshit plans, and now Rosa?

—Hey, not you, you don't have the right to talk about Antonio, on my mother's life, hey, show some respect, goddamn it!

—What, I don't have the right because I'm a whore? Well, for your information, he didn't care, Antonio, he loved me just the way I am, didn't judge me, yeah, came to see me all sweet, so cute, really kind, he wanted us to get out of here, away from all the crazy ass people like you!

—Bitch, you're lying, goddamn it, on my mother's life, you're lying!

—And this, what's this?

Margarine quickly leans forward to take a belt from under the mattress, on the buckle a Native American. She brandishes it like a trophy in front of Mouloud, dumbfounded.

—Holy shit, Antonio's buckle. What did you do to him?

—Asshole, it's your dealer friends who took him out. He wanted to give them their dough and get out and take off with me, but what he sold wasn't enough for them. He even stole from his parents for that. Antonio didn't have enough, they beat him up like sick assholes, and then they took him out behind the supermarket and injected him with the stuff ... We had a date ... The cops didn't even move a finger ... They couldn't care less about Antonio ... about me ... no one gives a shit!

She pauses and then starts to cry.

—Go on, get out, scram!

Hysterical, beside herself, clenched teeth, her face red with hate, she rushes toward Mouloud, who doesn't move, and pounds her fists with all her might on his chest. Next, she scratches his face and screams, unable to calm down. Mouloud steps back from the attack, gathers himself, and grabs her by the shoulders to calm her down.

—Cut it out, shit!

She spits on him, insults him, pushes him, kicks him, yelling. A black veil of anger blinds Mouloud, and images of his own suffering overwhelm him. His strength multiplies tenfold within seconds, a surge. He grips Margarine's throat with one quick brutal move. The image of the officer's boots beating down on him as he lay there on the ground. He's bathing in his own blood and begging for mercy. Rage intensifies in his hands, a noose, the fingers press even more intensely, and the suffocating words and sounds Margarine releases escape him completely. He needs quiet and serenity to regain his thoughts. He's vacillating between the present and his past suffering, the basement, the desert, Mouloud is going to the other side. He's forgotten that he's immobilized Margarine with an iron fist. He can see the officer brutally picking him up again and ordering him to get down on his knees, then everything becomes blurry ...

Margarine is no longer resisting; her upper body goes limp and falls alongside her body. Her head hangs to one side. Mouloud has avenged the months of feeling filthy, the humiliation and violence. He comes back to himself with the contact of the warm and viscous liquid running down slowly on his hands. Margarine's mouth is bleeding. He discovers a face frozen with an expression of horror. He lets go of her as you might dispose of a burning object. Deep nail grooves cut around his arms, the bruises reveal the futile attempts at resistance by the victim. He looks at her, lying on the ground, contorted. Her

Wilfried N'Sondé

open thighs form a broken cross, one leg is straight, the other points outward, her left arm is stuck behind her back, a bare milky white breast hangs outside the bra strap. He realizes that she's not wearing anything underneath her skirt. Margarine lies on the floor of the basement, inanimate.

Mouloud takes off, disappears into the night, trapped in the hood. A thick fog blurs his path, a desperate meltdown, no aim in sight.

SALVATORE MOVES SLOWLY toward the obsession that has been haunting him for a long time, determined to pay the price to have, if only once, the body in full blossom of this young woman he's been watching, with her ample thighs, her generous chest, and provocative strut. With some change and a bank bill, he can give himself the extravagance of a moment of human warmth. He goes by the closed supermarket, a night watchman in a dark blue uniform is on duty. On the other side of the little square, two men are smoking in silence. Salvatore goes around the huge pot of flowers in its pride of place on the roundabout, then he disappears into an alley, his cigarette going back and forth, at regular intervals, toward his mouth. He continues into the poorly lit alley with privet hedging. He raises his head and for a second takes note of the balconies encumbered with all sorts of diverse objects, stripped bicycles, engine parts, car tires, abandoned strollers. This tableau makes the neighborhood look like a whole other continent.

The taste of the flattened filter, hot at the tip, is getting bitter on the tongue. He crushes it as you would something that torments you. Salvatore imagines the little pieces of hidden skin, firm, pink. He has almost forgotten the velvety contact of Angelina's soft lips on his skin. When they were young and in love, she used to laugh a lot and her mouth was always stuck to his. He's going toward a presence, in hopes of tasting the desire his body is longing for. His simplest desires are orphans to him.

Imagine a blond comforter, moist, perfumes, savors, a family man caught between need and shame. Is she alone in the basement of the uninhabited building? He walks alongside the back of the building in complete darkness, the electric lamps and streetlights have been stolen and never replaced. The fifty-year-old pauses before the entrance decorated in multicolored graffiti, he lowers his head and exhales at length. Salvatore descends, after having verified that no one has seen him, then closes the door behind him, being very careful, and places a flat stone at the base of the door, between the wood and the ground, so that it can't be opened from the outside. A dim light in the back of the corridor guides his steps. He enters the room and finds Margarine's body motionless.

ONE SUSPECT REMAINS to be brought in. Mouloud Zayed was not at home when the police went by there. Witnesses confirm having seen him the night before, in the early evening, entering the basement of a building in the complex. Lieutenant da Silva and Captain Traoré are preparing to go over to project 6000 to verify the information they received:

—I've got a bad feeling about this, you know, Moussa, I don't like to go digging around in basements!

A half hour later, both officers get into their unmarked police car and head over to the location, followed by a small van from the national police force. Now stationed in the parking lot of building F, the duo head toward the basement. At the same time, police officers ward off curious and idle onlookers approaching before securing the perimeter with a red police cordon. Laurence and Moussa enter the basement, armed with powerful flashlights. They advance carefully for about ten yards, then turn left and stop dead in their tracks, shocked by what they discover.

At their feet, the lifeless body of a young woman is lying on the ground. The silence is sad and heavy. You can hardly hear the hissing sound of the wind howling through the staircase, a cold caress, as the door remains open. The girl seems stuck to the concrete, enveloped in an invisible shroud of dust, urine smells, and excrement. Margarine's body is stiff, stretched out in an obscene position, her crotch is wide open, gaping. Her blue eyes staring wide-eyed tell the surprise and full horror of the tragedy, her face, a terrifying mask. Death seems to have taken her to the height of suffering, limbs splayed, traces of the violence around her neck, her clothing ripped open, revealing her pale breasts, the blows from the previous night had left purplish marks in several places.

Pale, Laurence is overcome by nervous spasms, her legs buckle beneath her weight, nausea intensifies, she places one hand on her mouth, the other is looking for support against the wall to keep her balance. The seconds feel interminable, her eyes are riveted to the unbearable sight, she loses control of her bearing. The lieutenant rushes to the exit, a chaotic rush, the sudden urge to take in a breath of fresh air. She bumps into the cement walls and ignores her superior's injunction:

—Lieutenant, what's the matter with you? Shit, get it together, goddamn it!

She's choking, she needs to clear her head a minute, quickly get rid of the knot of bile coming up in her throat. Doubled over, Laurence stumbles in the staircase and, once outside, vomits, choking several times and coughing. While wiping her mouth and nose after blowing it, she responds to the agent approaching to inquire:

—Thanks, it's over ... It'll be OK, thanks ... It's going to be all right!

A few minutes to get her thoughts together, she avoids crossing the inquisitive gazes of the onlookers and colleagues who are worried. One of them asks:

—Lieutenant, what's inside?

—A girl has been killed ... A kid, twenty years old at the most!

Alone before Margarine's body, Moussa Traoré squats down and closes his eyes. The girl seems so young, almost still a child; she must have been gorgeous. The nakedness of her intimate parts bothers him tremendously, but he remains blocked, motionless, he doesn't cover her.

⁓

Laurence da Silva straightens out her clothes and goes back in to her superior. He breathes deeply, still shocked by the violence of the tragedy and preoccupied by the horrific turn of events. They're both silent before the young lady lying in the dust, with the mystery of the dried blood on the cement. The pain that can be read in the eyes of a girl, so young, triggers a profound malaise, the feeling of a life completely wasted.

⁓

Mouloud Zayed, he remains at large.

THE ANNOUNCEMENT OF the murder of Margarine shakes up the whole project, news of more violence, but this time, the vilest! The police confirm that strangulation was the cause of death of Marguerite Pinson. Her cranium had been damaged after several blows against the wall and the ground. She had not had sexual intercourse before her death. At the counter of the bar, the hypotheses run the gamut, the girl had apparently been killed by a dangerous psychopath or some serial killer:

—Given that she'd been a whore, she must have finally fallen on a real sicko!

The rumors recount the facts of an incredible atrocity. Margarine had been tortured all night long by a sadist with a criminal record. She had undergone unimaginable sexual abuse with various objects of different sizes. Everyone used their imaginations and their fantasies, the commotion drowned out the sounds of drink orders and the coffee machines at work.

In front of the supermarket, a neighbor tells Angelina that the little blond girl, her daughter's friend, the one who sleeps with all the men, was savagely murdered, they tore off her huge breasts and ate her genitals, like in the movies, definitely a real head case. You've got to absolutely barricade your girls in the house, this kind of person will do just about anything.

Angelina hurries to get home. Anna is probably alone in the house. On the way, the mother curses the rotten neighborhood with all its horrors that are killing the kids. She's now running while mumbling prayers to the Virgin Mary, asking her to protect, at the very least, her girls from the killer.

Once she's back in the apartment, relieved, she finds Salvatore at the kitchen window. He hasn't shaved, hasn't eaten, his jaw is clenched. Her husband seems overwhelmed by an immense fatigue. She recalls how he tossed and turned in the bed, he hardly slept and kept waking up in sudden fits, sweating, haunted by nightmares.

～

Images of Margarine, naked with her gaping sexual organ from which blackened blood gushed, terrorized Salvatore for a good part of the night. He saw himself running in the deserted streets, finding himself face to face with the figure of the deceased at each intersection. She kept turning around him, increasing in size before imprisoning him between her thighs. At that point, the family man ripped the sheets off his chest and got up before screaming. Angelina had preferred to sleep on the sofa in the living room.

～

Guilt is torturing Salvatore. He is going around in circles smoking cigarettes nonstop, back and forth, between the window and the table, his bed and the toilet. He no longer leaves the house. He thinks about God and mumbles the few prayers he can remember, his lips barely moving. Convinced he doesn't deserve salvation, he resigns himself to eternal suffering to pay for the heavy toll of temptation. His face is that of a man hardened by a life of poverty, manual labor, a spinal column broken from long-term unemployment, all weighing heavily on him. The tragic death of the young woman in all that filth in the basement. Huge tears mist his eyes and fall feebly on his cheeks … Salvatore sobs in silence, consumed by a longing to cry in his wife's arms, to have her console him so that everything can go back to what it used to be!

ALERTED TO THE agitation in the entrance to the building, Rosa Maria joined the discussion among the girls gathered in the hallway.

—What, you didn't hear about it? Margarine was found dead in the basement, some crazy shit, disgusting!

Yet another blow to the head, now her best friend was dead, turmoil, head spinning, adolescent girls' high-pitched squealing, screaming, and gesticulating in the air. A cascade of blurry images, her smile, a taste of full lips posed on hers, the sensation of escaping into the wheat fields, over there, Margarine and her stretched-out laughing fits, tenderness. The pain overwhelms her, she has difficulty breathing. The light suddenly goes black, she faints into the arms of the girl standing next to her. Her big brother is dead, yesterday her best friend, soon the *café au lait* baby in her belly. They place her on a step and try to revive her with gentle pats on her temples.

—Hey, come on, Rosa, wake up, you're scaring us now!

She eventually comes around, cries her eyes out uncontrollably, without saying a word.

—Holy shit, girls, we better take her back inside, she's about to lose it!

Together, they manage to carry Rosa Maria all curled up, her muscles tense, stiff, pale face, she's grinding her teeth, her jaw is locked. The shock has imprinted her face with a crazy expression, shortness of breath, speechless. She's carried and left on the steps to her apartment door. After ringing the doorbell several times, the others take off.

Angelina opens the door, her daughter falls right into her arms, they hold each other tightly. Overcome by the intensity of the embrace, Rosa Maria and her mother collapse together on the doormat and cry for a long time.

Standing in front of the window, Salvatore is still smoking, disconnected, his back slouched, his cheeks hollow. His eyes with dark circles are sunken into their sockets. Depleted of thoughts, he no longer sees or hears anything around him.

Rosa Maria doesn't know what to do anymore, torn between leaving with Mouloud for Bora-Bora and the abortion. Sonia stands firmly by her position, intransigent. It's time for her to go see her savior so that they can get out of here. If she keeps on doubting and hesitating, they're also going to wind up being devoured by the projects, this Hydra, killer of women, men, hope, a vampire that feeds itself off the blood of young people. She wants to see Mouloud and convince him to speed up the preparations, so that one day her child can prance along on a sunny beach, even more beautiful than Sicily, at the end of the world. She dreams of diving headfirst into the turquoise blue of the ocean, warm, transparent, shellfish with velvety shells, magnificent colors, a sensation of complete calm coming from the contact with soft tropical algae on her skin.

Mouloud has returned to his parents' home and locked himself in his room. The scene of the fight has polluted his head and keeps horrifying him, he's going crazy. His forearms are streaked with long, swollen scratches. Despite several washings, Margarine's blood, especially on his hands, persists, indelible. If only he could fall into a deep sleep then wake up and realize that all of this was just a bad dream. He hides in a corner of his room, sitting right on the floor, chin on his knees, his eyes glued to the door. He's imposed absolute darkness on himself as punishment, obsessed by the bright blond hair of his victim, a specter relentlessly hounding him. Mouloud is falling apart. Bora-Bora has completely disappeared from his mind, the beaches have become vast deserted spaces where balls of dust dance, no more bursts of laughter, nothing. His brain is faltering for good. Rosa is no more than a shapeless shadow, Antonio, a distant mirage. Mouloud's mind is saturated with information and images, all attempts to concentrate are failing. Short-circuited. When he tries to scream, to call out for help, no sound comes out. Sometimes still, words leave his lips without him wanting them to, an uncontrollable flow that surprises and frightens him. He's struggling.

Time has passed, it's probably morning, now he's alone in the apartment. Someone knocks. The force of the knocks and the authoritarian voices worry him. Mouloud is on his guard. Lost in the fog of his thoughts, a dark expression, evil, he grabs a knife in the kitchen. He opens the door and gets into a panic when he sees the uniforms in front of him. He waves the white weapon before the police officers, pushes the one who advances against his colleague, locks himself in and yells:

—I'm going to bleed you dry like sheep, leave me alone!

ROSA MARIA IS alone. Her friend Margarine is dead. Jason is in prison. Mouloud, still being sought by the police, seems to have disappeared. He's out of circulation. Gone, paradise island on the other side of the world with seafood on the menu, white beaches, head spinning from traveling crazy and intoxicating roads—it's all come to an end. Stretched out on the bed, her face buried in her pillow, alone in her room, she makes out blurry images of her little chocolate love walking clumsily between her lover and her along the neighborhood paths. She sees Margarine again smiling, hears her, bursting out laughing in the train cabin, romantic songs repeated in chorus before settling into the side aisles and kissing like lovers, the sun in their eyes. Some minutes of freedom, far from everything, a breath of fresh air in their lungs. The sky is pure, it bathes the countryside in sheets of gold, the landscape of Île-de-France is spectacular with trees lined up like sentinels of happiness in the immense yellow fields. Rosa Maria is a child again, the simple pleasures of childhood, hugs, tenderness that makes you feel good. She has a hard time holding back the tears, the neighborhood unhinges everybody. Margarine grew up on the streets like a wild plant, big, beautiful, and sensual in the middle of the grime on which she wound up lying forever.

Close to Rosa Maria, emptiness, an open wound, an uncertain future, now that the dreams have been punctured on all sides, evaporated into indifference and absence. Her newly spread wings have already been broken, she has fallen from the sky, all that remains is opaque mud all around her.

Her father is clearly drying up, he looks like someone being chased by the devil. At least he's leaving her alone. He's endlessly scratching his thick gray stubble, never saying a single word. Sonia no longer consoles her. Her big sister only asks that she kindly avoid yet another disaster, then she goes about her business.

—OK, good, now, Rosa, keep your nose clean, please, just don't make any waves, gotta just cut your losses!

∾

Rosa's chest has gotten shapely, full, the young girl notices it as she contemplates her reflection for a long time in the bathroom mirror. She sighs, she's barely been able to feel like a woman, and now she has to go to the clinic for an abortion incognito. A blade and local anesthesia are going to remove the fruit of the seconds of love with Jason. Rosa Maria has accepted putting her desire and her own will on hold.

Only yesterday, the little heart was beating timidly on the screen from the ultrasound. Fascinated at having created life by offering her body to her beloved, Rosa Maria was over the moon. Two days ago, during her lunch break, the gynecologist had examined her private parts, legs open wide on the examination table, her head leaning backward. Absent, she forbade herself to feel anything. At no point did the practitioner look at her; he merely examined.

ANGELINA GOES TO collect Anna, whom she has left for the day at a friend's place in the neighborhood. Suffering from persistent headaches, she left work a little bit earlier. The mother is tortured, so much tragedy in such a short time. She dreams of leaving project 6000 and wishes for the complex to be swallowed up by a lifesaving tsunami after she leaves. Her husband has lost the ability to speak, you would think he'd crossed an evil spirit in person. It's been two nights now that he's been screaming like a crazy person, making it hard for her to sleep. Rosa avoids her, elusive, and Sonia, who's looking pretty morose, is killing herself at work. Little Anna has tons of questions for which she has no answers.

—Karima, it's me, Angelina. Send down the little one, I'm in a hurry ... thanks again ... see you later!

Her index finger leaves the button of the interphone. Angelina adjusts her outfit and takes a breath, ignoring the clamor getting louder in the distance. About a minute or so later, her daughter arrives, flies into her arms, and covers her in kisses.

—Mama, Mama, Karima says the police are all over the place. Do you know what's going on? Apparently there are a lot of them.

~

Angelina almost jumps out of her skin. She starts trembling, and her migraine starts up all over again.

ROSA MARIA HAS had an anonymous abortion. She dresses in silence. The effect of the anesthesia is beginning to wear off, the pain keeps jabbing into her lower abdomen, she's bleeding. In the end, Sonia had refused to go with her:

—You're a real pain, Rosa, shit, I can't. I'm working while you're sleeping around with all these black guys! You're on your own now!

A gust of wind picks up right before Rosa Maria's horizon, a storm that definitively sweeps away Jason, the kisses in his aunt's apartment. The rays of light in her eyes have disappeared, the cherished baby is now gone. Sicily carried away in one sweeping embrace, the black sand from its beaches covers the entire world, November is here, the neighborhood she makes out in the distance is uglier than ever. Ever since the iron entered her private parts, everything has disappeared. Hope has run aground, its flowing nonstop from her belly. The obstetrician wiped away the sweat on her forehead before taking a breath and washing her hands. Rosa Maria is suffering, her body and her soul form one great affliction. Nothing left to see on the ultrasound screen, everything has been replaced with agony, starting from her knees and moving right up to the tears that have yet to be shed. Ten thousand white-hot needles torturing her abdomen and lodged into her thighs.

CAPTAIN TRAORÉ AND his colleague from the antiriot police are reviewing the situation. Moussa begins to question the methods being used. He doesn't like the cold and warlike tone of his counterpart, who wants to wrap up the whole matter as soon as possible. It will be up to the courts to determine the guilt of the young man being pursued, who still deserves some respect.

Police officers have been deployed around the building. A special intervention team advances slowly up the stairwell. The inhabitants of the entrance have been evacuated. A cordon is keeping the crowd at a reasonable distance.

The whole situation has left Moussa with a bad taste in his mouth. The young man, who will not be able to get away from them, remains a mystery to him. Why didn't he try to escape? The measures that have been put in place concerning this unstable person seem exaggerated, out of proportion.

﹋

Angelina and Anna cross the street quickly, right in front of the police car driving at full speed, blue police lights flashing with a deafening siren. It goes by so fast that it's impossible to make out Mouloud's parents, completely doubled over, in tears in the back seat. From the front seat, Laurence da Silva is holding the hand of the old woman and trying to comfort her:

—Don't worry, ma'am, it's going to be all right.

—My son didn't do anything, he's a good person!

Her husband is wearing a hard, cold mask, moist streaks on his expressionless face, the traces of tears. Laurence is taking them to the police station. She's going to record their deposition before handing them over to the national police force's psychological unit.

⁓

Rosa Maria is in pain, suffering with each step she takes to the bus stop. Her dashed hopes have left an emptiness in her head, solitude, despair.

—The suspect has just washed his face, his hands, and feet in a basin of water, he's squatting and reading a big book…

Moussa is distraught, he's thinking about sitting down for a minute. He would love to be able to explain to his colleagues that however guilty the suspect might be, this is a solemn moment for a believer. The captain is standing on stiff legs, stoic, just as much a stranger to his colleagues with whom he shares the three-striped card as the one who is submitting himself to God right in this moment.

The blood is pulsating like crazy in Angelina's veins, especially at her temples. That bad feeling she's been having since yesterday has now been confirmed. Something catastrophic is lurking in the air. She hastens her step, dragging Anna brutally by the arm, ignoring the child's complaining:

—Don't pull so hard, Mama, you're hurting me!

The mother makes out a gathering in the distance, the fear of yet another tragedy grips her in the stomach, her moist hands begin to tremble uncontrollably. Police officers in huge numbers are on a war footing, the tension is palpable, a tragedy has occurred.

Luckily, it's not the entrance to her building. Angelina is relieved that at least this time her family has been spared.

ROSA MARIA IS waiting alone under the bus shelter. Still, she feels neglected, abandoned, wounded, heading to the complex, returning to no life, humiliated.

Mouloud murmurs, he chants while rocking back and forth, the palms of his hands caress his face before resting delicately on his thighs close to his knees. He repeats these gestures again and again, a part of life, bracketed from the world around him. Mouloud prays for his parents. Eaten away by regret, he asks Rosa and the child she's carrying to forgive him. He submits to the Almighty, the only one who can forgive his mistakes. He swears that he tried to do the impossible before the situation got out of hand and became a crazy story, a real disaster... To the point of no return.

Mouloud is all confused, his ideas are getting all mixed up again. Margarine, resuscitated, kisses him on his forehead and caresses his cheek, she's wearing a necklace of tropical flowers, a light transparent sarong that barely covers her legs, a gold and silver piece of jewelry decorates her navel, she is beautiful. A distant voice comes to his ears and whispers: Indulge yourself, Get away, Discover Bora-Bora!

Margarine and Mouloud embrace tenderly, a fluid dance, barely swaying in the basement, they reconcile. Then Rosa and her son run toward them on a white sandy beach of the South Pacific. A warm, smooth voice out of nowhere announces in the mic:

—Welcome to Bora-Bora! The water temperature is perfect, dinner, seafood on a bed of coco leaves, and nonalcoholic cocktails will be served under the palm trees at approximately eight p.m.!

Mouloud doesn't hear the loudspeaker threatening, the police summoning him to surrender, he is surrounded, no chance of getting out:

—You would be well advised to cooperate . . .

Amid the confusion in his head, Margarine is dancing on the beach. The sound of the boots in the stairwell is dangerously gaining momentum. Mouloud is surprised to feel his pulse racing so fast, his palms are sweaty, he sees himself straddling a white horse over there in the desert, the sand is turquoise blue, the tide coming in and out . . . Project 6000 is disappearing into the calm of the waters.

～

Mouloud is unable to complete his prayers before the door bursts open. He has just enough time to catch a glimpse of the weapons and the helmets of the officers who rush toward him, as one of them maces him. Mouloud passes out, the world vanishes and suddenly drowns into a thick fog.

ANGELINA TAKES A turn to bypass the crowd, dreaming of just collapsing onto her sofa in the living room, to forget herself for a moment, close her eyes before taking a hot bubble bath of fruity fragrances. Then to dine afterward in the quiet and fall into a deep sleep. Anna climbs the stairs quickly to the second floor and, waiting for her mother at the doorstep, goes ahead and knocks:

—Nobody's home, Mama!

They enter, Angelina is immediately worried. Anna settles into the armchair in the living room and turns on the TV. At the edge of the open window in the back of the kitchen, there's a letter addressed to Angelina. Her fingers are trembling so much she has a hard time opening it. The text is brief:

She was still breathing when I got down to the basement. I recognized Antonio's belt and I went crazy. May God forgive me.

SALVATORE

Angelina rushes into their bedroom. It's empty. She opens Antonio's bedroom, then the girls', still nothing, and Salvatore is not there either. She stops for a minute, reads the letter she's holding in her hand again, and rushes outside.

—Where you going, Mama?

Angelina descends the stairs to the basement, enters the basement, and stumbles on a chair turned upside down. She feels her way for the light switch, the light goes on. Salvatore has hanged himself with an electric cord attached to a hook in the ceiling. His tongue is dangling from his mouth, giving him a goofy-looking expression. His stomach has sunk toward the ground, and he has soiled the pants he's wearing, held up by his son's belt. A yellowish stain has formed beneath him, and there's a disgusting smell. Angelina stares at the scratch marks around her husband's neck. The instinct to survive must have compelled him to fight before his passing. A part of Angelina dies right there on the spot, blown away by the nightmare of her husband suspended in the air. She recognizes the jacket, the shirt, and the black pants, fitting poorly now after so many years, the outfit he was wearing on their wedding day, back there in Sicily, on a sunny Saturday afternoon, an outdoor celebration that was filled with so much hope, at the foot of the mountain ...

THE BUS RIDE home to the neighborhood seems interminable to Rosa Maria, the torture continues, the agony of tiny metallic needles planted into a wound continues to torment her stomach. At the least break or sudden start-up of the vehicle, the pain becomes unbearable, running all the way down to her toes before shooting back up her spinal column and lodging itself in her spine. Amid the general indifference, she has a hard time getting up from her seat to get off. The young woman walks painfully toward the projects, doing her best to absorb the wave of shock that shakes up her whole being as soon as she puts her foot down on the asphalt. She moves along wincing, stops for a moment, and looks up.

A noisy agitated crowd blocks her view. There are vans and blue uniforms close to Mouloud's entrance. In the distance, a loudspeaker and a barely audible message, yet she is able to hear:

—Mouloud Zayed ... This is the police ...

Rosa Maria refuses to hear any more. The wound between her legs, the commotion in her ears, not a word from her mouth, the dried-up dream buried in her eyes, sweet revolt in her fists, she decides to turn around.

The young woman imagines light somewhere toward the horizon, she ignores the rectangular buildings at her back and the cold, moist wind that brings with it the bitter smell of exhaust pipes. Rosa Maria heads past the cars and trash containers, crosses the square in front of the supermarket, and takes off. She advances backward to distance herself from the grime and the concrete. The sky is black with dark clouds. Bitterness is doing a number on her, Rosa Maria is heading toward the unknown, she's not afraid.

⌒

A bus deposits her at the train station. While going down the steps, she stares at the tracks and hesitates a moment ... In the distance, the yellow headlights of a locomotive looms in the night. As it approaches, a fresh breeze blows through her hair and violently sweeps the platform. Weak in her bearing, she vacillates, closes her eyes, and rocks gently from front to back on the tips of her toes. The emptiness before her pulls her in.

Rosa Maria allows herself to be lulled by the rhythm of the monotonous motion, her eyelids closed until the train pulls into the Gare du Nord station.

So as not to miss out on the landscapes she will discover in the morning, she settles in comfortably into a window seat, in the direction of the moving mainline train that will take her far from the project 6000 cages. Anywhere. The final whistle blow rings out. With tear-filled eyes, Rosa Maria is dreaming.

WILFRIED N'SONDÉ was born in 1969 in the Congo (Brazzaville) and grew up in France. He is widely considered one of the shining lights of the new generation of African and Afropean writers. His work has received considerable critical attention and been recognized with prestigious literary awards, including the Prix des Cinq Continents de la Francophonie and the Prix Senghor de la création littéraire. He is author of *The Heart of the Leopard Children* and *The Silence of the Spirits*.

KAREN LINDO is a scholar of French and Francophone literatures and currently teaches and translates in Paris.

CPSIA information can be obtained
at www.ICGtesting.com
Printed in the USA
LVHW04s2218270818
588270LV00005B/1149/P